GEEKTASTIC

MARY FRAME

Cover design by Najla Qamber Designs
https://www.najlaqamberdesigns.com
Editing by Elizabeth Nover at Razor Sharp Editing
www.razorsharpediting.com

Geektastic

She needs a story. He's trying to escape one.

Annabel Moreland has promised not to leave podunk Blue Falls, Texas, until her little brother graduates. But she's about to lose the job she needs to support him, which means they'll end up homeless wretches, and it will be all her fault. Worse, she can't swing a cat in this town without hitting someone she would rather forget.

Unfortunately, the answer to this litany of problems comes in the form of an unforgettable, dead-sexy, cat-loving, shenanigan-directing trickster named Jude Parker. He's got enough secrets to fill the Mississippi, and she's on a mission to fish out every single one.

She just needs to do it without falling into his bed . . . again.

For Jenny Juchtzer and Georgia Vanderville, for a lifetime of friendship (and then some) despite the fact that I'm a giant weirdo most of the time. I love you guys <3

Chapter One

The more I know of the world, the more I am convinced that I shall never see a man whom I can really love. I require so much!

—Jane Austen, *Sense and Sensibility*

Annabel

EVERY TIME I go out of my way to avoid someone, they appear. Like magic.

Like dark magic from hell. Or in this particular case, like the devil incarnate.

Jude Parker.

Our gazes clash and then my eyes skitter away like they've been scalded, but his image is burned on the back of my retinas.

He's wearing a suit. Black jacket, stark white shirt, black bow tie. Which maybe wouldn't be remarkable, except this isn't a fancy restaurant or a wedding. It's a township meeting in rural Texas.

The Blue Falls High School cafeteria was an unlikely hellscape, but the city hall was unavailable because someone had flushed their dentures down one of the public toilets and they had to close for water damage. This was the largest available public space, equipped with plenty of uncomfortable seats, glaring overhead lights, and squeaky linoleum.

Jude should look ridiculous amid the rest of the over-sixties currently occupying the room in their beige and pastel shirts and slacks—they don't even seem to notice he's there—but instead he looks like he always does.

Relaxed. Unconcerned. *Delicious.*

The outfit is a stark contrast to his scruffy beard and long hair. The brief glimpse of his intense, bright blue eyes has my stomach twisting with nerves.

My first instinct is to run, but I can't. There's no getting out of this. The town council meeting every month is one of my only bylines.

"Annabel." I yank my gaze from the blue-eyed devil in the room. Rudy Quinn stands near the head table where the town council convenes, dressed in his perfectly pressed police uniform, the badge on his chest glinting under the fluorescent lights.

"Heya, Rudy." Everyone knows Rudy. His daddy is the district attorney. Plus we went to Blue Falls High near about the same time. He's at almost every event I have to cover for the paper. He's a bit on the awkward side, and on the round side, and pleasant enough, but it's hard to exit a conversation with him once it gets going. He's like sweet tea in the South: abundant and always available and too much makes your teeth ache.

"Covering the meeting for the paper?" His accompanying smile is wide and friendly.

I nod. "As I do. Anything good on the docket tonight?"

"Oh, you know how it is. We've had increased calls to the station about unidentified vehicles around town. Chief wants me here because we know it's gonna be a topic. He wanted me on hand to help reduce the paranoia and assure the public that there have been no increases in crime in conjunction with the sightings, no reports of any theft or the like, and we have things under control. We've increased units patrolling through town and are on the lookout for anything suspicious. He knows I'm the best person for the job, the voice of reason, so he's been sending me out on overtime almost every night this week. I'm really the best at—"

"Right. Yes. Of course you are." It's so rude, but I have to nip it in the bud or I could be stuck up here all night. He opens his mouth but I speak before he can. "Good luck. I'd better find my spot. Catch you later."

"Yeah, I'll catch you later," he calls after me. "Maybe we can get a drink or something after."

I step lightly through the senior citizens crowded around the front.

All the regulars are here. Mr. Gepson with his toupee and spiral notebook, pencil worn down to the nub. Elaine Kilgarriff dressed in her pastel pink summer dress and hat even though it's November. Mrs. Johnson with her ancient tape recorder—which is so old I don't think it even works anymore and yet she brings it every time.

I make my way toward the back of the room, avoiding where Mr. Jude Parker was last spotted.

Which is a mistake because he's moved. He's now standing at the back, against the wall, right next to my regular spot.

It's like he knew where I would be setting up. But how?

I almost turn around and find somewhere else to stand. But no. Righteous indignation fills me. This is my town. I'm not going to let him intimidate me. I don't care what he does.

I continue to the back of the room, giving myself a silent pep talk as I make my approach.

He's just a guy. No one important. Act natural.

"Annabel," he acknowledges, his voice low.

"Good, thanks."

As soon as the words leave my mouth, I want to snatch them back and swallow them down.

Jude is grinning and clearly enjoying every tortuous second.

"What are you doing here?" I ask, trying for a brisk professional tone that sounds more jittery than I would like.

I catch a whiff of his cologne—something manly and hot and a contrast to the cafeteria stench of old pizza and teenage angst. The citrusy smell ignites a flicker of a memory. Of being in his bed, curled up against him . . . but I ruthlessly quell the image.

His bright blue eyes burn into mine like he can read

every lascivious daydream I've ever had about him along with ones I haven't thought of yet.

"I'm surprised you have to ask," he says.

Crap. What did I ask?

"As you know," he continues, "I take my civic responsibilities very seriously."

Oh, right. His moustache twitches and I know he's smiling underneath it even as he talks about being serious. As ever, he's taking amusement from everyone and everything.

It doesn't escape my attention he didn't actually answer my question.

"Right. Whatever." I shrug my bag up higher on my shoulder and consider my options. I can't stand right here next to him.

Space. I need space.

"Enjoy the show," I murmur and walk on, continuing my path along the back wall a good fifteen feet away from where he's standing. His eyes burn into my back and I'm glad I wore the dark blue skinny jeans that make my butt look awesome.

Not that I care what he thinks about my butt. Not. At. All.

I pull out my phone and small notepad and set my purse on the floor and pretend to not watch Jude out of the corner of my eye when he moves to a table right in my eyeline.

He doesn't do something as simple as sit, either. He lounges, arranging his body like he's relaxing on a chaise longue instead of the hard plastic bench attached to the scratched and battered orange table that's been in this room since at least 1947. I'm pretty sure there's a carving of my name on the underside of that very table, next to where I drew a little heart with Chad's initials.

The town council members trickle in from a side door. The mayor, the city manager, and the secretary with her small typewriter all take their places at the table up at the front of the room.

The mayor calls the room to order, and it begins as it always does with a prayer to bless the meeting, followed by the pledge of allegiance.

Shifting from one foot to the other, I try my best to focus on Mayor Adams.

"As the Texas Open Meetings Act does not allow the council to respond to items not listed on the agenda, your comments will be duly noted by the council and forwarded to the appropriate department for prompt consideration."

Which means they will listen and likely do nothing.

Almost immediately, Eldon Dunbar gets up to discuss the installation of a stop sign "over by where the aliens were spotted at Gary Johnson's farm." Riveting.

My eyes, the traitorous bastards, linger on the back of Jude's head, trailing over the line of his shoulders in his dark suit. It fits impeccably, hugging his broad back like a perfectly wrapped present. A present should be opened. Presents can't lie around, wrapped for all eternity. It's like they're asking for it.

I glance down at my phone. It's not on. I forgot to turn on my recorder. Smashing a finger over the button, I burn a hole into the back of Jude's head with my eyes.

It's not my fault he's got this thing, this sexy-vibe thing.

It doesn't matter that he's hairier than a komondor and somewhat resembles a yeti. Even with all that hair covering ninety percent of his face, he's still got this crazy, all-enveloping presence. It's like pheromones or . . . I don't know, invisible lust tentacles.

I've never seen him at any of the other meetings, and this definitely isn't his type of deal. He's all about parties and bets and making money off his "babies," as he so affectionately refers to the college kids he uses to supplement his income.

As far as I'm aware, he's lived in Blue Falls for about six months, but even in that short time, he's become something of a legend. A master of games and wagers, a purveyor of parties and shenanigans, and also my brother's former roommate.

"I would like to talk about the government listening to my phone calls every Sunday." We've got a new commenter. Elaine Kilgarriff.

I suppress a smile.

The NSA isn't really interested in the secret ingredient for your fried chicken, Elaine.

"They park down the street in their van. They're trying to listen to my conversations and they've been walking around behind my house late at night. One of them snuck in through my doggy door and used my shower."

Mayor Adams coughs.

"And then they made a sandwich. I know it wasn't my Eugene that did it because they cleaned the utensils and wiped off the counter after, and he ain't never done that."

Mayor Adams tilts her head toward Rudy, who clears his throat from his position to the side of the committee.

"Ma'am, we've been alerted to the potential presence of suspicious vehicles and we're working tirelessly day and night to ensure they don't pose any kind of threat."

Jude shifts in his seat, once again drawing my attention.

Is he sitting slightly straighter? Leaning forward a smidge?

Rudy continues, "We do have more people residing in Blue Falls than ever before due to the new mining ventures outside town. A lot of them have families visiting for the upcoming holidays and the parades, which Blue Falls is renowned for. I would like to personally assure you that no one will be listening to your calls or harassing anyone in this town on my watch. Or, you know, attempting to burgle your sandwich materials."

Elaine nods and toddles back to her seat and the next Blue Falls resident gets up to talk about something inane.

I take notes for another thirty minutes while John Nottingham complains about his neighbor's tree overgrowing his fence and Mr. Gardiner talks about the drainage problems on the city side of his property, but my gaze continually finds its way to the back of Jude's head.

His stupid, attractive, hairy head.

Eventually, thankfully, Mayor Adams ends the meeting. I bend over for my purse, packing up my notes and tape recorder. When I glance around again, my eyes automatically locate Jude. Now he's near the door.

The fact that I'm so aware of him makes my jaw clench.

He stops to empty something from his jacket pocket into the trash and then, after a quick glance around, slides out the door.

It's an innocuous enough move, but something about it sends curiosity thrumming through me.

Just what did he throw away?

I stop by the exit and peer down into the receptacle. There's nothing obvious in view, but it's a narrow opening and the bag is black and dark.

God dammit, I'm even getting fixated on his trash? This is why I need to stay away from Jude Parker. He's dangerous to my sanity.

Doesn't change the fact that I'm ten seconds from becoming a full-fledged Dumpster diver.

"Do you want to go have a drink at Bodean's?"

I jump damn near a mile.

"My treat?" The overly enthusiastic question comes from Rudy.

"Aw, I wish I could but I'm meeting Fitz for supper. Sorry."

This isn't the first time Rudy has asked me out. He asks everyone out. It's what he does. I've never said yes and a twinge of guilt slips through me at his hangdog expression.

"It's okay." His shoulders droop. "Maybe next time." He walks out the door.

It's not that he's a bad guy, it's that I would rather not hear him talk about himself for two hours.

The bite in the air is a brief shock to my senses, as is the darkening night. The days are getting shorter as winter settles in and brushes its gentle fingers across this side of Texas.

I shrug on my sweater and focus on my next step and *not* on Jude Parker.

The excuse I gave Rudy wasn't a lie. Fitz and Reese, my brother and his girlfriend, are home waiting on me. Well, they saved me leftover pizza. That totally counts.

I'm living with Fitz, but she's there a lot. I don't mind. I love Reese. She's awkward and smart and sweet . . . but I think I might keel over from all the PDA going on around our apartment. It's like a never-ending puke fest of love.

If I had known moving in with Fitz would turn into watching them spew sweetness on each other twenty-four seven, I would have lived in a box next to the H-E-B with ol' Roy.

I would charge her rent if she weren't already renting a room from . . . Jude.

And there he is again, my mind running back to him like a pulled tooth you keep tonguing even when you don't want to. And since *I do* want to tongue him, it's a terrible, terrible metaphor.

I turn the corner to the school and run into another wall.

One that wasn't here before.

A tall, muscly, man wall.

Jude. I know it's him because his hands on my shoulders transmit a signal through my body like I'm fiber optics and he's sex moving at the speed of light. My entire being focuses on the heat of his fingers touching me.

I jump back and throw up a wall of indifference,

something that will protect me from Jude and his magic lust tentacles.

His sleepy eyes smile at me, the cool blue belying the heat in his gaze.

"What are you doing?" I ask.

"I wanted to offer my services as an escort to see you safely home," he drawls, emphasizing the word *escort.*

I smirk in an effort to appear unaffected, but I'm afraid the effect is more of a lumpy grimace. "I'm just fine on my own but I thank you for your concern." I walk past him, setting a brisk pace.

His lengthy strides have no problem keeping up with my shorter gait. "I would like to express my apprehension, despite your obvious ability to care for yourself, as there are mercenaries about as per Ms. Kilgarriff's testimony. Safety in numbers. I have thoughts only for your welfare, being a gentleman and all."

"Well, shouldn't you be walking her home then?"

"Maybe I should. I could check on her if you like, but I don't think I have the address of her residence."

I snort. "Right. A gentleman and a civic leader. I'm not buying it. Why were you really here?"

"If I recall correctly, I asked you that very same question."

He did. The first night we met, at his house.

I was there at the behest of my editor, who wanted to do a story on illegal gambling on campus. Jude's games.

"I told you why I was there. To check on Fitz." My brother, who had gotten himself embroiled in one of Jude's little betting schemes. Fitz had gotten kicked out of his friend's house, and Jude had lured him into a competition to rent a room.

Jude tsks. "A lie that doesn't improve itself upon repetition."

"If you're so certain you know why I was there, why do you bother asking?"

"Because I don't know why you were there. If I knew why, I wouldn't ask. I know you had reasons other than those you alluded to."

"Maybe I'll answer your question if you tell me what business you had at the township meeting. You didn't speak on anything."

He grins down at me. "Darlin', were you watching me?"

"Don't call me that."

He called me that before. In his bedroom. The lights down low, his hands wrapped around my ribcage, holding me tight, his voice in my ear, his lips running over the sensitive lobe.

He smirks, as if he knows the affect he has on me and enjoys it a little too much.

I'm not going to get any clear answers from him so I continue walking. He keeps up and we move in silence down a side street that will take me to my apartment—the opposite direction of Jude's house near the university.

We sidestep a youngish couple taking their dog out for a walk. They wave and exclaim, "Beautiful night, isn't it?" as they pass, holding hands in domestic bliss.

"They seem nice," Jude says once we're out of earshot.

I snort.

"We could have a dog together one day," he continues.

I hold back a laugh. "I would not purchase any kind of canine with you. Ever."

"You're right. Felines are definitely better, and I'm not sure Mr. Bojangles would appreciate having to compete for my affections."

"No competition here."

"So I take it you haven't reconsidered my offer of dinner?"

"Answer is still thanks but no thanks."

"Just checking. I had thought all of the hostility and avoidance of my general person might indicate a rekindling of your prior interest." Humor tinges his voice.

I stop walking and turn to face him. "I'm not going to change my mind. I'm not interested in a relationship. If you want to pursue a physical relationship . . ." I run my eyes down the suit. Dammit, he's even hotter up close. It doesn't help that I know what's underneath. I take a step closer. "Those are terms I might be amenable to."

A relationship with Jude would be a threat to my sanity. But a nice roll in the hay? That I could handle.

My bravado falters.

Maybe.

I hope he says no.

Because the truth . . . the truth is Jude probably wouldn't want anything serious with me. Not if he knew the real me. I'm an unworthy imposter, undeserving of his regard, but I tuck the thought away like a secret diary slipped beneath the mattress. Or porn.

He searches my eyes, his mouth set in a line until one

corner pops up. "I'll keep waiting for you to come around to my way of thinking."

"It's gonna be a long wait." I spin on my heel and march away.

I need to breathe in air he doesn't penetrate, but he follows, keeping up the pace until I've reached the corner where the sidewalk turns into my apartment building.

"Y'all take care now, ya hear?" I say in the best, politest, stickiest-sweet voice I can muster, the one I learned to use on cranky teachers and customers, and turn to go, but he stops me with a word.

"Annabel."

His voice is deep and rough and I turn and face him, like I can't even control it. He's standing there, hands in his pockets, eyes bright even in the dying light, and as inscrutable as ever.

He opens his mouth, shuts it. Opens it again.

It's a move so unlike the self-assured and confident Jude I've come to know that I'm momentarily shocked.

"Be careful," he finally says.

I blink. What is he warning me of? But then he turns and walks away.

I stand there, staring after him for a few long seconds before turning on my heel and huffing down the sidewalk.

Jude is a mystery I've long wanted to unravel. He's hiding something. I know he is.

But more disturbing to me is how much I want to spend time with him. How much I actually enjoy the banter.

He's dangerous to the safe little bubble I've built. One poke, and it could pop.

Chapter Two

The power of a glance has been so much abused in love stories that it has come to be disbelieved in. Few people dare now to say that two beings have fallen in love because they have looked at each other. Yet it is in this way that love begins, and in this way only.

—Victor Hugo, *Les Misérables*

Jude

I STOP at the corner and turn to watch as Annabel huffs herself into a right tizzy, stomping off toward her apartment. This isn't the first time I've made her angry.

The first time, she was rescuing my cat.

Mr. Bojangles, spoiled feline extraordinaire, has a penchant for climbing himself into precarious positions and then wailing for assistance. It's his way.

Two months ago, a party was just getting started at my house. I was otherwise distracted with preparing for the event, and Mr. Bojangles had once again got himself stuck up a tree.

She was wearing a dark wrap dress, more fitting for the office than for a college party. Said wrap dress lifted slightly as she stretched up to liberate Mr. Bojangles from the low-hanging branch from which he could absolutely jump but preferred to sit and howl for a rescue. My gaze snagged on a brief glimpse of creamy thigh. Not much, but enough to tighten my chest and other parts of my anatomy not worth mentioning without offending delicate sensibilities.

I made my way through the throng of revelers taking up a majority of the space in my backyard—most of whom were more scantily clad, yet not as appealing as my feline rescuer—and came to a stop maybe ten feet behind her. She turned, Mr. Bojangles in her arms.

Our eyes met.

Now, I'm not one for flowery prose, but it wouldn't be overstating to admit that first glance carried weight. Heavy as a dead preacher. Whether it was the weight of a future enemy or lover, I still have yet to determine.

Heart-shaped lips, dirty-blonde hair, eyes the color of the smoothest whiskey this side of Kentucky, and the lushest body I had ever seen in my life.

"I see Mr. Bojangles got himself into a right pickle. Thank you kindly for coming to his rescue." I put on the mask I always wore in these situations and offered her my best humble, yet charming grin.

Mr. Bojangles started up a loud purr, louder than the

conversations filling the yard, and set a dainty paw on one voluptuous breast.

Lucky little beastie.

Her brown eyes, the color of a steamy cup of hot cocoa on a winter day, narrowed on me. "Is this your cat?"

Now, I wasn't exactly expecting her to fall at my feet. And being a gentleman, I would never intimate that every woman I smiled and flirted with was required to reciprocate, but I'd be lying if her serious tone didn't somewhat deflate my confidence.

"Yes, ma'am." I kept my voice light.

"And this is your house?"

There was a sharpness to her words, something piercing like a blade and penetrating like a probe.

I cocked my head, an intuition I'd learned to trust cautioning me to proceed with prudence. "For now."

"You must be Jude Parker." She mimicked my head tilt. "I've heard weird things."

"But you have heard of me." I grinned again, but she just lifted a cool brow.

Attempting to disarm, I offered her a flourishing bow. "In the flesh, madam. And who am I having the pleasure of conversing with?" I held out one hand to take hers.

"Annabel Moreland." She lifted her free hand reflexively and then used it to hold Mr. Bojangles tighter, ignoring my proffered fingers.

I let my hand drop. I knew who she was. The sister of my new roommate. I knew this because I wouldn't allow someone to live here without running a thorough background check. Drastic times and all that.

I knew all there was to know about Fitz. And consequently, Annabel. On paper, anyhow.

She stroked my cat and viewed me from under her lashes. "Can you help me understand something?" She smiled and the sudden shift to politeness had my hackles rising. Miss Annabel Moreland was not one to be trifled with.

"I'm at your leisure, Miss Annabel."

Her gaze shifted and focused on me with a shrewdness I could not have anticipated. "You're clearly too old for this scene, yet hosting a myriad of college parties."

Her eyes flicked up and down and I knew what she saw: overlong hair, beard, silk robe covered in cats. Ridiculousness. As intended.

Before I could respond to her observation, she kept going.

"You've got this whole devil-may-care, reliving-the-glory-days stereotype down to a T."

An act I was proud of. But her astute observation that it was just that, playing a character, sent a spark of worry trailing down my spine. She couldn't possibly know the truth.

"It's all very . . . clever," she continued. "But why? What are you hiding?"

So she didn't really know anything. The thought brought relief but also something else. Under her unflinching gaze, a miniscule crack formed in my thick façade. In the past six months, not one person had bothered to inspect too closely or ask any questions or think I was anything other than what I chose for them to see.

A spark of respect flickered to life in my chest. And understanding. Annabel was an observer of people, much like myself.

She was brash and bold and confident, and yet when I stopped to really watch her posture and gaze, she was not as unaffected as she'd like to seem. She held and petted Mr. Bojangles like she enjoyed having something in her hands to absorb her nervous energy.

Nonetheless, she watched me, waiting for me to respond, her jaw tight.

Not as calm and knowing as appearances would have led me to believe. She was hiding something, too. Likely not any kind of major secret, but . . . something.

"Why are you here?" I asked.

"You didn't answer my question."

"Because I have nothing to hide and nothing to answer. Do you?" I kept my tone light.

She blinked at me. "Fitz is my little brother." Defensive. She worked at the paper and since the simplest explanation was usually correct, my guess was she'd come thinking she could get some kind of story.

I watched her and waited, not speaking. It unnerves people. The quiet can be too much to bear in most of polite society. Especially Southern society, where one is daily smothered in proper etiquette.

Annabel was no exception. Her eyes darted to the side and she licked her lips before she came to some sort of conclusion and then met my eyes and lifted her chin. "I came to check up on Fitz to make sure he's not getting into a questionable situation."

"Trust me, there's nothing worth questioning here."

"I'll be the judge of that."

I extended my hand again, this time gesturing at the frivolity behind me. "As you can see, we are all merely players on this grand stage. Might I interest you in some refreshments while you enjoy your evening?"

"Uh-huh, right, Shakespeare." She took a step closer and straightened her shoulders. "Whatever you got going on here, if you mess with my brother, I will end you, you hear me?"

A slow smile spread across my lips, and it wasn't even an act. "Loud as a katydid in the middle of July."

Mr. Bojangles squirmed in her arms, and she put him down. He wove between my feet, purring.

Someone shrieked. Behind us, Beast was picking up one of the babies by the scruff.

I grinned. "It appears the celebration is about to get a proper launch. You let me know if you need anything, darlin'." I winked at her and turned away.

"I'm not your darling," she called out.

No. No, she was not.

She was a mighty fine distraction, though. Which, unfortunately, was not something I needed.

I didn't need it when we first met, not the first night, not the night I could have had her in any and every way possible—physically, at least—and certainly not now.

But I want it. And to emphasize the point, here I am, watching her enter her apartment building and making sure she gets inside safely before turning and continuing my own stroll home.

The walk is nearly a mile, but I don't mind the crisp

night air and having a chance to glance around the homey neighborhoods. It's always smart to be aware of one's surroundings.

I pass a couple kids on their bikes, yelling at each other about being late and getting in trouble. A black cat in a window spies down on the street. A couple blocks later, two neighbors discuss the weather over a row of hedges separating their property.

They wave and call out greetings as I pass.

I didn't know towns like this existed in real life until Grace led us here, but now I reckon I don't want to leave. I never had a home, and something about this town sure feels like one.

Maybe it's just Annabel.

She shouldn't feel like home. She's like a fragile bird with a sharp, sarcastic beak.

But there's something there. She's beautiful, of course, but it's more than that. She cares about Fitz. She would rather be anywhere but here and yet she stays for family. She's loyal. She's been hurt by something and it's making her defensive and I can't help but want to knock down every wall she's built.

I know what it's like to be scared.

By the time I reach the house, people are milling about, waiting to get in. I lope up the front walk and they clear a path for me.

"My man!" someone yells.

"Babies! Sorry for the delay, but your honorable host has now arrived." Once on the front stoop, I bow, donning my persona like a flamboyant cloak.

People clap me on the back as I move through the

front door, where Beast is collecting the entry fee. He takes up nearly all the space in the doorframe, silently taking funds and handing out poker chips in return. He lifts one dark, thick brow and I respond with a nod.

Communicating with a mere glance.

And now it's time to focus on the present.

Tonight I am the master of games. It will require very little interference on my part, which has been my main intention as of late. Grace has me stretched too thin with her tasks. Things are coalescing, gathering steam, and I'm not sure if I can keep up with her plan. If only I knew what her plan was.

The parties will have to be reduced significantly.

The backyard sold the house when I was seeking a rental. It's large, stretching back nearly an acre with a wide swath of grass in the center—perfect for nights like tonight.

Beast, Fitz, and I spent all afternoon stringing up colorful lights around the trees and bushes that encase the yard, casting glowing embers of light over the tables. Each table is set up with a different game—like a casino—except instead of roulette and poker, we have Connect Four, Go Fish, and Scrabble. Each of the players, all my babies having paid for their chips on their way in, will be able to cash out at the end of the night.

There will be many winners tonight but as they say, the house always wins.

The yard is full of coeds dressed to the nines. They mingle around the patio in suits and tuxedos, sparkling dresses and jewels. It's over the top and ridiculous and the story of my life for the past six months.

Someone nearby hands me the megaphone.

"Babies!"

The one word, uttered with a subtle mixture of humor and fondness, is enough to have the whole crowd clapping and aiming their rapt attention right at me. The master of games.

"It's a true pleasure that y'all have seen fit to join me tonight."

"I've got some pleasure for you right here!" an overly exuberant frat boy yells from the front row, and the crowd laughs.

"I know babies, I know, calm yourselves. There are more than enough shenanigans to go around before we say good night."

Once the cheers have subsided, I continue. "What we have for you tonight is something new. Something different. This isn't your local fraternity casino night. Oh no, babies. This is Jude Parker's Fun and Games Extravaganza!"

They go wild.

"It's everything you've ever dreamed and more. Don't be shy. Make your way through each table if you want. Beast will be on hand to give out more chips as needed and he will tally your winnings when you're ready to leave. Don't drink and drive, and tip your waiter because the champagne is on me."

The pronouncement is met with the largest applause yet.

More than a few babies are working off favors by playing cocktail waitstaff tonight.

Beast's looming form catches my eye as he moves into

the previously designated position over at the corner of the yard. I meet his eyes and, after a nod in his direction, yell into the megaphone, "Let the games begin!" I throw up my hands and, with impeccable timing, Beast pulls the string attached to the system of needles and balloons we set up earlier. A series of loud pops fills the night air, shooting a mess of colorful confetti down upon the entire party to gasps and laughter. The babies cheer and flood the yard.

I grab a flute from a passing waiter and step off the porch onto the yard to make a round before I can safely disappear.

An excitable jock gets handsy with a lady at the Operation table and I give Beast a heads up with a wave and a shake of my head. A lady playing checkers attempts to slide her opponent's chips into her bag and I pull her away and tell her to play fair or she'll be out.

Beyond that, the night is progressing swimmingly.

Before I can escape the yard to get to the more important work, I'm waylaid at the edge of the grass.

"Jude." I don't even have to look to know who it is. The nasal tone belongs to one of my regulars. She wraps her talons around my bicep, the sensation stinging even through my long-sleeve shirt and suit jacket.

"Hello, Melindra." She's a sweet young lady, a bit on the insecure side. She has a bet with her friends that she can get me into bed but I'm not that easy. Said friends stand a few feet away, trying to be nonchalant, but I know everything that happens under my domain. She's not a bad sort. I've been trying to let her down gently, to little effect.

"Wow." Her eyes pop open in a move too dramatic to be sincere and her hand on my arm tightens. "You look amazing in this suit. Did you dress up for me?"

I ignore her question. "I have some business to attend to. If you'll excuse me, madam . . ."

But I'm not going anywhere because as if sensing my imminent departure, like sharks in the water smelling fresh blood, her friends walk over and now I'm surrounded.

"Where do you work out at?" one of them asks.

"Did you buy this online?"

"You are so hot. I love your beard."

I'm no more than a piece of meat.

"Babies, have you played Uno yet? It's my favorite game." I turn them over to a table where a regular named David and one of his buddies are playing. "David is a king among men."

He's not. He's entitled and egotistical, but I'll call him anything if it will help extract me from this conversation.

I hand them some extra chips on the house, sneak out of the circle once they get to talking, and head over to Beast.

"Keep an eye on the ladies, will you? Make sure Mr. David doesn't get too comfortable. I don't know him well enough to leave him unattended."

Can never be too careful. And like they say, if it's got tires or testicles, it's gonna give you trouble.

When I glance back, though, the three ladies are surrounding David, and his brows are lifted near to his hairline. "Although I'm not sure who we should be more worried about."

I pat Beast on his massive shoulder, reaching up to do

so, as he is nearly seven feet tall and a behemoth of a man.

Moving through the house, I'm only stopped a few times since most are out back, and I finally, finally make it into the back of the house to my own personal space.

I engage the locks, including the extra ones I had installed after Annabel went snooping through my things.

Mr. Bojangles is lounging on my bed, sleeping, but he wakes up upon my entrance and stretches a delicate white paw in my direction.

I pull off my jacket before picking him up and holding him to my chest, carrying him over to the closet where I store my workstation. I pull the system out, clicking on monitors as I go. There are cameras set up everywhere around the house, both inside and out, so I can keep an eye on the festivities.

Beast is a prince and a giant, but his lack of communicable speech lends a complexity to our situation. And one can never be too cautious.

With Mr. Bojangles purring in my lap, I check the secure messaging website where Grace has been leaving periodic notes of a most cryptic nature.

Nothing.

I hope she gets the cash I left in the trash can at the high school. I don't have any idea how she has been moving about town without being spotted, but I imagine she's been sneaking into more than just Elaine's house to enjoy showers and sandwiches.

Left to my own devices, I search community pages but there's not much online. Blue Falls itself is about ten to twenty years behind technologically. Most of the government offices still use paper files and CD-ROMs.

There are some emerging signs of social media—neighborhood-watch-type apps are growing in popularity, and the university students are somewhat adept, but that's about it.

My inbox dings with an encrypted message.

There she is.

Tomorrow night she wants me at the middle school—all the way on the other side of town. To pick up something in the band room.

I've already secured a vehicle, knowing it might be needed. Plus it doesn't serve to use consistent methods of transportation on a regular basis, or to use the same paths. Routine is dangerous. And with the people at the town hall meeting talking about suspicious vans . . . not as much of a long shot as one might think.

This whole venture has been a struggle. Even though we've been here for months, people in small towns are more paranoid than even I am. Helpful if you're a local and in the know, but when you're an outsider, you're not quite one of them.

It would be useful to have a local on my side, but it's hard to know who to trust and it may not be fair to involve someone who doesn't want the complication.

Annabel might like the complication. And it would behoove us to have someone in the media on our side, except . . . I'm afraid her negative inclination toward my general person would be a hindrance and I could never do anything to put Grace or Beast in harm's way. They're all I have.

And yet, even more concerning—Annabel is all I want.

Chapter Three

I am no bird; and no net ensnares me; I am a free human being with an independent will.
—Charlotte Brontë, *Jane Eyre*

Annabel

FITZ'S TEASING voice carries out to the hall as I'm walking in the front door. "I still don't understand. Say it again?"

Reese's quieter, higher tone meets his. "The acceleration is the derivative of the velocity function."

"Yeah, doesn't help. But you sure are cute when you talk like that." Fitz laughs, the deep chuckle of someone completely satisfied and in love.

And then there is silence. And then the unmistakable sound of lips smacking.

Ew.

I turn into the doorway of the kitchen slash dining area—big mistake—and then immediately cover my face with both hands. "Must you do that in here?"

They're sitting next to each other at the rinky-dink vinyl table. Fitz has pulled her chair close enough so her legs are between his and he's leaning into her space. And they are absolutely making out.

I groan. "I'm so, so sad for my eyes right now."

"It's not like we're naked." Shoes squeak across the linoleum and then Fitz tugs my hand from my eyes. "Stop being such a prude."

I give him a death glare, level three since we're only teasing. "It's not prudishness preventing me from wanting to see my brother dry humping his girlfriend where I eat my meals. It's basic hygiene." I set my purse on the counter. "Where's my food?"

"There's leftover pizza in the fridge."

I do a happy dance all the way there. I haven't eaten since lunch, which was sometime before noon. I went straight from the office to the township meeting.

"Momma wants you to call her."

"I'll call her tomorrow."

He frowns at me but doesn't push. I've been saying the same thing every time he tells me to call her. I don't have the energy for it.

"How was the township meeting?" Reese asks. There are textbooks and papers spread over the small surface. She's dressed casually, her typical jeans and T-shirt. The shirt reads, *Obstinate, headstrong, girl.* A *Pride and Prejudice* shirt Fitz got her for their one-month anniversary.

"It was fine." I shrug and put the cold pizza on a plate before sticking it in the microwave.

"Anything exciting happening around town?" Fitz asks. "More alien sightings in Mr. Johnson's cornfield?"

"Not this time." I smile and lean against the counter. "Just your classic case of weirdos patrolling the neighborhood in creepy vans and listening to Elaine talk about her secret fried chicken recipe."

"A matter of national urgency," Fitz says with a laugh.

"Oh, and Jude was there," I mention super casually. "So that was weird." I'm way nonchalant.

No one responds to my statement at all. Crickets.

The microwave dings and I pull my plate out. "He was wearing a suit. And bow tie."

"He looks mighty fine in a suit." Reese packs her books into her bag.

I sit next to her at the small table. "You don't think it's odd?" I'm totally breezy.

Reese shrugs and Fitz watches her with a small smile, not even paying any attention to me or the conversation.

I frown. This is not progressing as expected.

"It's casino night, so he was probably dressed up for the festivities. Oh, that reminds me." Reese's eyes shift to Fitz. "Will you pick me up from the library after your track practice? I'm loaning Jude my car tomorrow night."

"Of course." Fitz smiles at her, his whole face lighting up as they hold eye contact for way too long.

It's so . . . exposed.

Gross.

"What does he need your car for?" I ask.

She shrugs, uncaring, her eyes still locked with Fitz.

"You're just going to let him take your car without knowing what he's gonna do with it?" I persist.

Her gaze finally flits to mine. "It's not like he's going to commit illegal activities or something."

Humph. "You don't know that."

"What is it with you two, anyway?" Fitz asks.

"I haven't the faintest idea what you're referring to." I take a huge bite of pizza and chew slowly so I don't have to respond right away.

"Nothing. Uh-huh." His mouth firms into a skeptical line. "You're full of it, Annabel Lee."

I give Fitz the death glare, kicking it up to level five, chewing with a bit more vigor. "There's nothing going on with Jude and me."

He rolls his eyes.

"I wouldn't walk across the street to piss on him if he was on fire."

"That's what I'm talking about." He points at me. "If he means nothing, then why all the animosity? You know what they say about love and hate: two sides of the same coin."

"There are no coins. I'm ambivalent."

I'm lame and a terrible liar and I know it. Therefore, a subject change is in order.

"What are we doing on Thursday?" I ask Reese. We have a standing date to try something new every week—something outside of Reese's comfort zone. It was her idea. She was a social recluse before meeting Fitz and now is on a mission to make up for lost time.

We've done ice-skating at the hockey rink a town over, a painting class at the small art museum with a bunch of six-year-olds, and ballroom dancing at the senior center. I get dragged along with her because she has no other friends, something she's been attempting to remedy every time we go out, but most people think she's a bit of an odd duck. She is, but it's one of the things I love most about her. Besides, I kinda like having her to myself. Everyone else in this town sucks.

"I was thinking archery."

"We don't have to drive outside town again, do we?"

"I convinced Granny to buy the target and bows and arrows." She grins at me. "She was really into it, actually."

I snort. "I bet." Reese's grandma will likely use it as an excuse to collect enough artillery to outfit an entire army unit. The woman is as wily as a coyote in a chicken coop.

"They should be delivered in time, and there's plenty of room on the farm to set it all up."

Reese's family home isn't really on a farm, but there is a barn and lots of open space. There aren't any animals in the barn, though, only moonshine.

"Speaking of Granny," Fitz says, "are you coming with us for Sunday supper?"

While I would love to spend time at Granny's, she is totally in love with Jude and I haven't wanted to risk running into him. "No. I'm busy."

They exchange a glance but then ignore my lame excuse.

I proceed to eat my dinner in relative silence while Fitz and Reese talk and tease and act all cute and generally drive me batshit crazy.

It's not that I'm jealous. I'm not. If anything, I'm worried about what will happen when the honeymoon phase is over and real life creeps into their dreamlike romance. I don't want to lose Reese as a friend because my dumbass brother screwed it up somehow.

I wash my one dish while they go into the living room to watch TV. Or pretend to watch it.

Then I follow them into the living room and throw myself in the faded recliner while they snuggle on the love seat. But I can't even focus on the cheesy sitcom because they keep giggling and whispering to each other.

"I've got an early meeting tomorrow." I stand from the chair, hoping they get the hint. "Good night, y'all."

"Good night," they call out as I walk away.

Once safely ensconced inside my room—with it's own bathroom, thank the lord for small mercies—I take a deep breath that isn't choking in romantic bliss and set about brushing my teeth and getting ready for bed.

I have a routine. I brush my teeth while staring at the bulletin board on my wall. It's cluttered with random poetry from E. E. Cummings, Emily Dickenson, and Sylvia Plath, mixed with literary quotes and one solitary picture from my semester at UT Austin. I have more, but I've hidden all but the one of me standing outside the "Greetings from Austin" mural on South First. I was only there for a semester. I wanted to eventually apply for their MFA program in writing, but it wasn't meant to be. At least not yet.

The early meeting wasn't only some excuse to escape the happy couple. We do have a weekly meeting at the paper and I've got to write up the town hall meeting before ten, when we send everything to the printer.

I am grateful for the job, even though small-town

papers are about as exciting as staring at the ground in the dark. It's a good job, even though I don't exactly love it, and it pays the bills. Who loves their job anyway? That's why it's called a *job*.

And Fitz no longer has to live at Jude's, which means it's easier for me to avoid him.

Fitz lived there for only a couple weeks before moving in with me. He couldn't live with me at the time because I was rooming with a couple of friends from college who had just gotten married. There was no way all four of us could have lived together. *I* didn't want to live with the lovebirds, but I had to wait for an apartment to come on the market before I could move out. Fitz's sojourn at Jude's worked out well, even if he ultimately lost his room there to Reese, because I needed the time to save up some money for first and last month's rent. And even better, it gave him the chance to meet Reese. Now they're nearly inseparable, though at least they are mature enough to see that living together after knowing each other for two weeks would be a bad idea.

I get into bed and kill the lights, shifting in the soft sheets and trying to get comfortable.

Laughter permeates the thin walls and I roll over and punch my pillow a few times to fluff it up.

They really seem happy together.

With that thought, something inside me clenches, but I shove any thoughts of a bearded man in a suit way down inside the cave of my mind and try to sleep.

AFTER HITTING snooze on my alarm three too many times, I'm rushing to get out of the house. Late. No time to make coffee, have to pick some up on the way.

I fly through the doors of the Finer Diner, across the street from the paper. I worked here all through college and know the entire staff like family.

"Cathy, I need coffee to go like ten minutes ago." I'm hopping from one foot to another, like if I make a full stop, everything might crash around me.

"I got you covered. You can pay for it at the end of the week." She's already moving behind the counter to grab the carafe and filling a to-go cup.

"You are a lifesaver." I glance down at my watch. I have three minutes until I'm officially late.

Someone sitting at the counter next to me clears her throat on a strangled cough and I glance over. I stop my weird hopping and everything inside me stills.

Taylor.

She's gazing at me with wide eyes, like she's as shocked to see me as I am to see her.

I avert my gaze and focus back on Cathy.

"You want sugar, darlin'?" she asks.

"No, it's fine. Thanks so much, gotta run." She hands over the coffee and without another word I'm out the door so I can breathe again.

"STAN, what have you got for the weekend edition?" Bruce is the editor of the *Daily Blue*. He's nearly seventy with white hair and an even whiter moustache. He always wears cowboy boots and says things like, "yer darn tootin' " and "I can tell you a thing or two about a thing or two."

The building is old and small. We have our meetings in the reception area. Behind the front desk is where the staff works, a set of three blue-toned cubicles. There's only one separate office for the editor. Even the bathroom is a simple one-holer in the back. The break room is barely large enough to fit one table with four chairs and a single coffee pot.

"I have a piece on the new restaurant," Stan says.

He just wants an excuse to go drink since it's a bar and grill.

"How many words?"

"Five hundred thereabouts."

Bruce nods.

Jane the receptionist taps her pen on her notebook. It's what she always does before she wants to speak. "They're starting auditions for *A Christmas Carol.*" She doesn't actually write any articles. She mostly formats, copy edits, and sends everything to the printer.

"Who wants it?" Bruce's gaze lasers at me but I don't bite.

Mike volunteers to cover it, plus he has the new cases at the courthouse, usually neighborly disputes, loitering charges, jaywalking, etc.

He starts droning on and on and my thoughts flicker back to the night before, when Jude told me to be careful. What was he talking about?

And why do I care? Why does he keep peppering my thoughts like an overspiced steak?

Maybe I need to get laid. Get some bad sex so I can remember why it's all a terrible idea. Stringless, unsatisfying sex. Yep, sounds great. Especially since all I've ever really known are awkward fumblings in the dark with men I knew wouldn't be around for long.

I glance around the assembled group.

Stan is the closest to me in age, maybe ten years older. He's not terrible looking, if you don't mind the beer belly and receding hairline.

He belches and then shifts and glances around to see if anyone noticed, and I avert my eyes.

Maybe not.

Also, ew. I really am getting desperate.

"I can cover the parade next week," Mike puts in and Bruce assigns him the coverage.

"Speaking of the parade, Annabel, how's it going with the public opinion surveys?" Bruce levels me with a squinty-eyed stare that he thinks makes him look like Clint Eastwood but really makes him look sleepy.

"It's going. I also have the write-up from the township meeting to put in."

"Uh-huh. How many respondents so far on the parade question?"

It's a point of contention within the community. There's a Turkey Parade and a Holiday Lights Parade within a couple weeks of each other and they're both in November. Part of the population thinks the light parade should be moved closer to the Christmas holidays. Another segment thinks it should remain as it is since it's tradition. And the rest think the two parades should be combined because the Turkey Parade is basically a bunch of glowing turkey floats and balloons and very similar to the light parade anyway.

I glance over my notebook like the number on the page will magically grow before I have to answer. "Three."

It's not my fault.

Bruce comes up with these boring questions, like, What's your favorite winter activity in Blue Falls? What new businesses would you like to see make their homes in Blue Falls? How do you think the mayor is doing? That last one had me tied up for an hour while I listened to an angry constituent go on and on about the state of affairs and how the new mines being run outside town ruined everything and are only here to line the mayor's already fat pockets. Then when I tried to take his picture to accompany his statement, his eyes darted around and he yelled, "I won't be captured!" and ran off.

Bruce's bushy white eyebrows lift. "Three?"

I nod.

The entire room falls silent. I half expect a tumbleweed to blow through.

Finally, Bruce nods. "We'll talk later."

Then he has Jane recap our assignments before the meeting breaks up.

Stan corners Bruce to talk more about his article and I escape to my little cubicle to power up my computer and get things started for the day.

Maybe Bruce will forget about the whole having-a-conversation thing.

I take a breath. I was incredibly lucky to get this job. The last reporter left for New York and an opening basically dropped into my lap. It helped that I'd kept an eye on the place from across the street when I was schlepping burgers at the Finer Diner through college, and that Bruce went to high school with my parents.

I log in and open a blank document to start on the township meeting write-up.

For a second, I stop and stare at the white page.

I used to love a blank screen. It used to mean a fresh start. Endless possibilities. No limits. Hope flashing in every blink of the cursor.

Now it means writing the riveting details of Prudence Brown's prize-winning roses, the newest flavor at the Frostee Freeze, or the latest play showing at Blue Falls High.

I've given up on old dreams. They can't pay the bills, and every time I chased them in the past, I got knocked back down to earth.

I'm still staring at my computer, my heart suspiciously heavy, when Stan comes back to his desk. A breeze of excess cologne and stale coffee wafts by as he plops down in his cubby next to mine, chair squeaking.

"You're up, Anna Banana." He smirks.

I hate it when he calls me that and he knows it, so I ignore it. "What do you mean?" I sort papers on my desk and sit up straight, trying to appear important.

"Bruce wants to see you in his office." Stan is grinning at me like he can't wait to listen in from the break room like everyone does every time someone's in Bruce's office. The walls are so thin you can hear nearly every word in the bullpen.

I roll my eyes at Stan and march toward Bruce's office like I have nothing to hide.

And I don't.

Bruce's office has the same muted-blue carpet and beige tones as the rest of the building. There's an old chair that smells like cigarettes and moldy paper. I choose to stand after he shuts the door and sits at his desk.

"You wanna talk about why you're struggling with the opinion pieces?" His voice is flat.

"What do you mean?"

"Come on, Annabel. Don't piss on my leg and tell me it's rainin'. We've talked about this before. You don't take this job seriously."

"That's not true. I've been working really hard. I'm doing the best I can."

Maybe if I tell three different lies, he'll believe one of them.

His brow lifts. "If getting three people to respond is your best, maybe it's time to cut your losses and find a new horse to ride."

"What do you mean?" My voice emerges on a high squeak. I clear my throat and cross my arms over my chest. "You said I'm a great writer."

He nods. "You're good with words." He leans his elbows on the table and steeples his hands. "I know you think this town is as country as cornflakes, but if you want to make it in this business, you need to prove you have what it takes. Journalism isn't like it was twenty years ago. You gotta work harder than a funeral home fan in July no matter where you're livin'. And you gotta take every job seriously. Even the surveys."

I don't know what to say so I stand there stupidly. I don't want to be a journalist. But no one knows that except me.

"There are other people in this town who would love to work here."

My ears start ringing. "Are you . . . firing me?"

"No." He sighs. "Not yet."

"Yet?"

"I'll give you a month probation. But you need to contribute and give it your best. I know you hate the routine articles, but come up with something new. Wow me."

I nod. This whole conversation sucks. I want it to be over. Mostly because . . . he's right. My face is warm and tingly and I can't meet his eyes.

I don't take this town seriously and now I'm going to end up a jobless, homeless, talentless wretch.

When I turn to leave, he speaks at my back.

"I know you can do this. You have all the markings of a great writer. You just need to put yourself out there more."

Saying nothing, I shut the door behind me without looking back and make a beeline for the bathroom.

Stan and Mike step into my path.

"Nice work there, Barbara Walters," Stan says.

Mike chuckles.

I ignore them both and keep walking.

Once safely alone with the door locked, I take a few minutes to splash cold water on my face and breathe deep. Maybe Bruce is right. I'm being a snob. I can find a good story no matter where I'm at or what it's about. I need to focus on the here and now. I just need to . . . put more energy into it. Do the hard work. And focus. Isn't that the mark of a great writer? Tenacity in the face of insurmountable odds? Even if it's not what I want deep down?

I head back out to my desk, head high, but it doesn't really matter because Stan and Mike are gone already anyway.

At my computer, I pull up a file where I keep all my ideas.

I run down the list, discarding most and adding a few new thoughts from last night's township meeting, trying to stay positive. Sometimes even the most innocuous leads can lead to something. I think.

Once I've narrowed it down a bit, I eye each option more critically.

The crop circles at Mr. Johnson's.

No. Aliens are overdone anyway.

Creepy vans moving around town.

Has potential. Maybe there is something to it. I could creep around town and find them myself. Knock on the window, maybe. But what if it's as simple as Rudy said? More people in town, nothing to worry about. I need something good.

My eyes move over the next item on my list. Jude Parker.

Damn his eyes. His name is on the list next to the campus gambling line item from a meeting two months ago, and something buzzes in my head.

It was actually Bruce's idea. He had gotten wind of the campus gambling and thought there might be a story.

Since I had gone to Blue Falls U and graduated only a year ago, I was the only one who could blend.

That's how I found out Fitz was involved in said gambling and living with Jude Parker.

When I told Bruce the deets, he was interested in Jude himself and who he was, where he'd come from, how he had gotten involved in the gambling, and why the cops weren't more concerned about it. I mean, there hadn't been as much as a noise complaint.

We did some digging, but he had no trail. Nothing on him. Like a ghost.

I teased and argued with Jude to try to get him to spill hints about his past, but he always eluded my questions.

I even snooped around his place but didn't find anything useful except he definitely has more computer equipment than your average citizen needs, and his level of tech doesn't fit with the appearance he's trying to project. It's definitely a façade, but to hide what?

I ended up writing a lame piece on the ethics of campus gambling because the cops didn't care about a little wagering—I mean, the frats have casino night at least three times a semester—and there really was nothing all that interesting about Jude except the fact that he's hiding something, including a six-pack underneath that beard and those weird cat robes. But no one was interested. The fine readers of the *Daily Blue* want to hear about where the next Rotary Club meeting will be, why the stoplight on Main Street is broken, and what the one-screen cinema downtown will show next.

But maybe I can follow this thread. Just once more. If

it doesn't pan out, I'll drop it. But I need something to keep my job, to keep a roof over my head and Fitz's.

I know Jude's using Reese's car tomorrow night. It would be easy to follow him. I can do this. My goals will not be swayed by a hot dude with sexy lust tentacles.

Not ever again.

Chapter Four

Sing in me, Muse, and through me tell the story of that man skilled in all ways of contending
A wanderer, harried for years on end . . .
—Homer, *The Odyssey*

Jude

I RECKON I'm being pursued.

Annabel would be less conspicuous if her fan belt weren't shrieking like a hog being tied at a barnyard picnic.

Maybe I should attempt maneuvers to lose her, but I find myself curious about what her intentions are and why she feels the sudden need to tail me through town when she's been working so hard to avoid me.

I want her to find me, even if it's just to fight me.

She's the Gamora to my Star-Lord.

The Leia to my Solo.

The Dean to my Sam.

A few blocks away from the middle school, I pull down a darkened side street and park under a tree. I keep to the shadows, weaving through the residential neighborhood. People are home in their living rooms, watching sitcoms and movies and eating popcorn. Wouldn't that be nice, to have no more to worry about than what's on TV and what to make for dinner?

There's some kind of soiree transpiring at the school tonight. The lot is full of family vans and sedans. I avoid the area near the gym doors, where the thump of music spills out into the night, and instead make my way to the side entrance, where I've been informed the door to the band room will be left unlocked.

I reach the prescribed location without incident, turn the scuffed metal handle, and slide it open on a long creak.

The room is empty. Moonlight through the windows highlights chairs and music stands stacked on the sides of the large open space.

I check the trash can, as that tends to be Grace's modus operandi, and locate a lumpy object under the bag lining the can. An envelope.

There's a flash drive inside. I glance around the room, making another cursory check for any additional items, but nothing else is out of place. She doesn't typically leave more than one item anyway, but it never hurts to check. I toss the envelope, and while I'm walking out the door, I slide the drive into the front pocket of my pants.

Hopefully, it contains information about her future

plans and endeavors, but I doubt it. She doesn't want us to get hurt. She's always been too damn honorable for her own good. And knowing Grace, leading me on this wild goose chase is all good fun for her.

A flash of movement catches my eye. On my right, behind a tree about fifteen feet away.

There are two options here. The more likely one is that a blonde-haired, brown-eyed goddess who was already on my tail has found her way to my location and is currently awaiting my next move. Option two is more sinister and connected to Grace and perhaps those dark vans that were a topic of conversation at the town hall meeting.

Better to be safe than attacked.

Tense, but not wanting to let on that I know someone's there, I pat my pockets like I've forgotten something and slink back into the building, down the hall, and into another classroom. I have to pull off the screen, but then I shimmy out the window, coming out behind the tree that hides my watcher.

When I discover my tail, a smile presses at my lips. From behind, her blonde hair glints in the darkness, calling like a beacon.

Annabel.

Moving as silently as Mr. Bojangles, I approach her from behind.

She's peering around the trunk of the tree, her head turning this way and that, likely wondering where I've disappeared to.

She's completely unaware I'm behind her.

She spins on her heel and lashes out with her fist, right at my solar plexus.

I'm caught off guard, thought the blow would have been much worse had I not pulled back at the last second. I lose a bit of breath but manage to reach out for her arms before she does any more damage. Mistaking my reach as aggression—at least, that's what I tell myself—she blocks my hands and skims her foot behind my legs, sending me to the ground. I grab her by the shoulders this time and yank her down with me.

"Annabel," I wheeze. "It's me."

She either can't hear my attempt to push words out of my lungs or doesn't care because she's on top of me—and not in the way I've always imagined.

She pins my arms down, her hair a messy halo around her. I could break out of this hold with ease, but I don't want to. She's a lioness. A beautiful, skilled warrior. An amazon.

She's breathtaking.

And so I laugh, which clearly pisses her off, and her hands flex on me tighter.

"What are you doing at a middle school dance?" she hisses. "Are you some kinda pervert?"

I take my time answering, regaining my breath and enjoying the feel of her over me. "I could ask you the same question, darlin'."

"Don't call me that. And don't you try and turn it around on me, Jude Parker. What are you mixed up in? Why are you here?" Clearly not concerned about any retribution I might administer, she liberates one of my arms and uses a free hand to pat at my front pockets. "What did you put in here?"

She must have observed me putting the drive in my pocket. I'm not sure what's worse, having her on top of me, legs squeezed around my waist, or her hand roaming around my hips.

Said hand stills when it comes across the hard, small lump of the flash drive.

I shift underneath her, making no moves to stop her roving hand. "I've got something a little bigger for you over to the left."

"Ha ha ha, you sure about that Parker? That's not what I remember."

I recognize the verbal tongue-lashing for what it is. She's still hurt about when I wouldn't sleep with her.

But it was for her own good. When we're together I want it to mean something more to her than a quick release, which was all she was interested in. Catch and release. Not happening.

She sticks her fingers into the lip of my pocket and that's when I take the upper hand, rolling until she's underneath me. I hold her hands in one of mine, a gentle bracket over her head since she's already squirming.

"I find this position is more appealing at times for the ladies. The angle can be better."

"Tease," she says, just before she tries to head-butt me.

I jerk back and narrowly avoid a forehead to the nose. And then my wild cat relaxes every muscle, allowing herself to go limp.

I'm in serious trouble.

I don't relax my hold. "Annabel. I'm going to get up. Please don't hurt me."

Her shoulders start shaking. Now she's the one laughing.

"Oh, you find this situation humorous?"

I take a deep breath to brace myself before pulling back and up, stepping away, prepared for another sneak attack. But she doesn't attack.

She rolls to her feet, hair flying, cheeks flushed with exertion.

She's so beautiful. My brain transforms into a browser window with 1400 tabs open, gets overwhelmed, and goes into shutdown. I'm momentarily dumbfounded. So much so, she's waving the flash drive at me for a full three seconds before I realize she even has it. "So. What's on this?"

"You don't know what you're getting involved in."

"Then tell me."

"I reckon I can't do that."

"Why not?" One hand on her hip, cocked to the side.

"It may not be safe."

She rolls her eyes. "I know you're not who you say you are."

Everything inside me stills. "I am Jude Parker."

She shrugs. "So you say."

"Who do you think I am?"

"Nope. No way. You spill first. Then I'll give you this back."

My mind rushes through possibilities and potential outcomes. I have no one to talk to except Beast, and Beast doesn't talk. I want Annabel in my life, despite her prickly demeanor. Plus she's a local. Maybe she could help. Maybe I could offer her a story in exchange for her assistance.

I won't tell Annabel everything, not yet, but I could give her some information and then let her choose her own path. Sneaking around like she is, she could fall into something worse.

It doesn't take me long to decide. If I keep her close, maybe I can keep her safe.

Laughter distracts me for a brief second as a door opens, and music along with some preteens spill out of a door down the way. I tug her by the elbow back behind the tree, blocking us from view. "We should go somewhere to speak on this privately."

"Nope. Somewhere public."

"You don't trust me? You've been in my room alone before, if memory serves."

Instead of answering, she purses her lips at me. "Meet me at the Finer Diner. They're open till eleven and usually pretty slow at this time of night." It's close to nine. "I'll give this back if I decide your story is worth it." She holds up the thumb drive. "And no lying."

"I've never lied to you." Withheld information, surely, but never lied.

We walk in silence away from the school. She's parked right behind where I left Reese's VW.

Without a word, we get into our respective vehicles and I follow her to Main Street.

I have no doubts Annabel was following me to find a story. She's been digging into my past, sneaking around the house. She even broke into my room before.

I guess there's just one question, really. Can I trust her? Even if she doesn't trust me?

I know she's not indifferent to me. But she buries everything so deep I'd need an excavator to find her real feelings. Because with feelings come pain and fear. What happened to make her afraid of life?

The Finer Diner is nearly empty. There's only one other car in the lot. I follow her inside, through a haze of greasy burgers, onions, and coffee. She leads me to the rear of the restaurant. I slide into the red vinyl booth across from her and against the wall in order to keep an eye on the patrons coming and going.

She watches me for a few beats, her brown eyes dark and inscrutable. "Talk."

I take a breath and adjust the silverware in front of me so the napkin is perpendicular to the table edge. "I'm going to tell you everything I can." I speak slowly and carefully before meeting her eyes directly. "But first I would like the liberty of posing my own questions."

"What kind of questions?" Her arms cross over her chest.

"Nothing untoward, I assure you."

Her lips purse. "I'll be the judge of that."

Our gazes clash for a long moment and I try not to focus on the pink lushness of her lips, remembering the feel of them.

"Fine," she says finally. "But I reserve the right to not answer."

I nod. She wouldn't answer if she didn't want to anyway, and I wouldn't press her into anything uncomfortable. "Why do you work for the paper?"

She blinks and her head tilts to one side. "What do you mean?"

I fiddle with the butter knife on the napkin. "Let's just say I'm questioning your journalistic integrity before I spill all my secrets. If I'm giving you something, I need a little something in return, and I'm not asking for much."

She watches me carefully, but before she can respond, the server comes over with a couple of waters.

"Annabel, darlin', how are you, honey?" The waitress side-eyes me. She's in her midseventies, her white hair pulled back under a bandana. She's wearing a matching red-and-white-checkered apron with *Finer Diner* scrawled on the front.

"I'm good, Cathy. How is it going tonight?"

So she doesn't care when other people call her darlin'. Her aversion for the term must be specific to me.

"Oh, you know how it is, there's a football game, so we won't get any traffic till the game lets out. Who's your friend?"

"Jude, Cathy. Cathy, Jude," Annabel monotones.

But Cathy is all smiles. "Oh, I just love that name, reminds me of the song."

"Thank you kindly, ma'am, but I don't believe you are nearly old enough to remember any songs with my name in the title."

She giggles and pats my hand. "Oh, bless your heart, you just made this old lady as happy as a tick on a fat dog."

Annabel is scowling at me and I widen my smile.

"Annabel, you've found a good one here. And I'll tell you, I know you are gonna be a highfalutin writer someday, but we sure do miss you round these parts." She leans in my direction, like she's letting me in on a secret. "Annabel here was the best when the soft serve was acting up. She could get in that machine and work it like you wouldn't believe."

Annabel's scowl has deepened and she's turning a delightful shade of bright pink.

"I bet she excelled at many aspects of her job."

"Oh yes, the customers loved her. She could memorize orders no matter how many there were in a party, and on busy nights, she was a lifesaver. All while she was in school, too. Girl has more stamina than any of us, I reckon."

"Stamina is an important ability," I add, for the sole purpose of watching Annabel's face turn scarlet.

Cathy nods at me. "When you're on your feet all night, you bet your bottom dollar it is."

Annabel coughs. "Thanks, Cathy. That's so nice of you. Uh, can we get two burgers and fries with chocolate shakes?"

"Oh right, of course, honey. No problem." She takes our menus and gives us both a beatific smile, patting Annabel on the hand before waltzing off to the kitchen to put in our order.

"How much stamina do you have, darlin'?"

She narrows her eyes on me. "Don't call me that. I think there was something else you wanted to talk about?"

Still smiling, I hold up my hands in supplication. "Right. You were telling me why you want to be a highfalutin writer someday."

She bites her lip and plays with the napkin on the

table in front of her, flipping up one edge with her thumb before adjusting it to be perpendicular to the edge of the table. The same way I have mine set. I suppress a smile at her subconscious mimicry.

"I . . . I've just always been drawn to writing."

It's a true statement, but I can't shake the sense she's hiding something. And so I give in to my intuition and give her a little nudge. "Do you even want to be a journalist?"

She blinks at me. "What do you mean?"

Definitely hiding something. "Why do you want to be a writer?"

"Why does that matter?"

Defensive. I adjust tactics. "What made you think I'm not just your friendly, neighborhood party guy?"

Her shoulders relax slightly. "The computer equipment in your closet. It's a high-tech setup. Why would you need all of that?"

"You really are a snoop, aren't you?"

She shrugs and takes a sip of her water, her eyes darting away.

"I'll answer your question if you tell me how do you feel about ethical grey areas. Things that are morally . . . ambiguous."

"What do you mean?"

"What if someone does something illegal, but for a good reason? Do you think exposing them is fair and ethical when the person could go to jail for it?"

"Like what, specifically?"

I wave a hand. "Like someone stealing a loaf of bread to feed a hungry child."

She blinks. "I don't think someone would go to jail for taking a loaf of bread from the grocer."

"Let's say it's a lot more than a loaf of bread but for just as good a reason."

Her head tilts as she considers the question. "I guess it would depend on the details of the situation."

"So if I were to tell you about something with moral ambiguity, something that could potentially hurt someone I care about, would you keep those bits to yourself?"

Her mouth thins and she taps the table with a finger. "I don't want to get anyone in any kinda trouble, but if you've done something illegal and you're expecting me to—"

"No. Not me." Our eyes lock. "I'm trusting you, Annabel. I'm trusting you to understand how good people sometimes do what they must to survive and protect those they love."

She doesn't counter right away, thankfully. I won't get her full cooperation until she considers all the implications of what she might be getting herself into. And I need that cooperation, not just for her sake, but also for Grace's.

She nods and her expression is smooth and serious. "I understand what you're saying. I can keep certain aspects confidential as long as it doesn't hinder the integrity of the story."

"It won't."

"Fine then. I won't betray your trust."

The bell over the front door gives a jaunty jangle and we both turn and watch a group of teenagers spill into the diner, laughing. They head to a booth near the front window, and once they're seated, I turn back to Annabel to find her watching me with somber eyes.

Now it's my turn to take a drink of the water in front of me. Where do I begin? I suppose I'll stick to what's relevant, for the moment.

"I came to Blue Falls at the direction of a friend who may be in trouble."

Her head cocks to one side, throwing a long strand of blonde hair onto her cheek. I tighten my hand to avoid reaching out to brush it away. "A friend?"

A pause fills the air between us, lingering a moment, then two. "Grace."

Annabel blinks rapidly and then takes a sip of her water, the only sign my words have any significance. "Grace?"

"Yes."

"You . . . don't know if she's in trouble or not?"

"It's a bit complicated."

Her eyes roll so hard they might tumble out her head. "Break it down for me and we'll see if I can comprehend."

"Grace has"—I spread my hands on the table—"unique talents."

One elegant brow lifts. "Really?"

"Before you start feeling jealous," I can't help but smile at her clear displeasure at the mention of another lady, "let me assure you that Grace and I are merely friends."

"I wasn't jealous," she clips.

Well, now I must tease her a little. "I understand it might be difficult for you to hear me speaking of another woman, but I promise she's more like a sister."

She groans. "I don't care, Jude. Get to the point. What are these unique talents?"

Still smiling, I continue. "You mentioned seeing the setup in my closet. What I have, what I can do . . . I'm like a toddler compared to what Grace is capable of."

"So she's, what, a hacker?"

"Yes, but it's more than that. She's not just some script kiddie." I glance around the diner. The teens over in the corner are using their straws to blow wads of napkin at each other. Cathy is yelling something at the cook in the back. I lower my voice anyway. "Grace has the capacity to crack into the most secure servers. She's obtained back-door access to literally every alphabet agency you can think of and a few more most people don't even know exist. She can get in and out without detection as easy as you or I walk through a door."

"Okaaay."

"She's here in Blue Falls, and she's been sending me messages periodically, and I've been trying to assist her with her ventures here."

Her eyes are shrewd. "But you don't know what she's up to?"

I wince. "I have an inkling."

"Which is?"

"I'm afraid I'm unable to give you more information unless you decide to help. If you're all in, I'll trust you. But I can't risk Grace by revealing too much until you're sure you want to be involved."

"Fair enough. But I have more questions and you've

got to give me a smidge more before I can make any kind of decision."

Cathy comes over with our plates. "Here's two classic burgers and fries and milkshakes." She takes the items from the tray she's holding and sets them in front of us along with ketchup and some extra napkins. "Anything else I can get y'all?"

"Thank you, ma'am. You're so good at your job we have everything we need before we even have to ask." I smile at her.

She pats me on the shoulder. "You let me know if you need anything, sugar," she calls behind her as she walks off.

We dig into our food for a few quiet minutes. A couple of the kids push buttons on the jukebox and strains of "What's New Pussycat?" fill the diner.

"What are the rest of your questions?" I finally ask.

"Why did Grace guide you here? To help her? If she's so good, why does she need you?"

"Grace is a genius. She can do nearly anything with a computer. But she's also just a kid."

Her brows lift and she stops midchew. "Wait. A kid? How old is she?"

"Seventeen."

She watches me for a full ten seconds and then goes back to her burger and we continue our meal in silence. I glance up at her periodically, watching her chew on the information I've given her.

"Your question to me, about the moral ambiguity." She's moved on to her fries, dipping one into her chocolate shake before tossing it in her mouth.

"What about it?"

"Grace. She's participating in illegal hacktivist-type activities. Yeah?"

"More or less. You should probably know, it's not only for herself. Or for me. She also has a brother whom she's taken care of her whole life. She feels responsible for him, for a variety of reasons."

"He's younger than her?"

"No, actually, he's a couple years older, but he's got a bit of a problem with communication and Grace is his only real family left. I consider them both family even if we aren't blood relations."

She stares at me, realization crashing over her face like a wave. "Grace is Beast's sister."

Chapter Five

When falsehood can look so like the truth, who can assure themselves of certain happiness?
—Mary Shelley, *Frankenstein*

Annabel

JUDE NODS at my proclamation and pops a fry in his mouth, all nonchalant, like he's not dropping one bomb after another right in my face. "Grace had been using her skills to . . . appropriate funds from other hackers who had nefarious intent. At least, that's what she had been doing before we became acquainted."

"So Grace was breaking the law in an effort to support herself and Beast?"

He wipes his mouth with his napkin and settles it back down on the table, leaning forward. "She didn't really have many choices. She and Beast were too young to get any kind of legitimate work. When we left Valdosta, I was seventeen. Grace was only nine and Beast was thirteen. At that point, I was able to step in and help support us so she could cut back on some of her extracurricular activities."

I consider his words for a second. "But not cease them altogether?"

His smile is rueful. "Not quite. Old habits die hard, and Grace obtains too much personal satisfaction from besting bad guys. But I did convince her to go to school—online—and that's when she also started working on a special project. One that I think is the reason she ended up here in Blue Falls."

Curiosity eats at me, but I know he won't feed me all the details quite yet. "I just don't understand why any kind of hacker would need to come here. Nothing exciting ever happens in Blue Falls."

He shrugs. "The program Grace was working on would be beneficial to many. Government agencies, businesses, and also those with more malicious intent wanting to get an edge on their competition."

Malicious intent? If there's something illegal going on . . . "Why don't you go to the police?"

"I was specifically advised that may not be a viable option."

I snort. "Really? Like someone on the Blue Falls PD is a bad guy? The cops in this town aren't exactly IT professionals."

"Be that as it may, I don't have enough details at this juncture to be making those kinds of decisions. I took the liberty of reviewing the background checks conducted on everyone who works at the local station, but they're all squeaky clean. Which is what I would expect, considering most people of a villainous nature would excel at covering their tracks. I'm trusting Grace. Whether that choice proves itself to be a poor one remains to be seen. Although she's never steered me wrong before."

"Before? Has she done this before?"

He shakes his head. "While Grace is endowed with a strongly independent nature and in the past would sometimes take off for a day or two, it's never been like this. And to be quite frank, I'm worried about her."

"Why?"

"Grace is the smartest person I know. She can do nearly anything with a computer, but she's still just a kid and she needs help with more . . . basic needs. She'll get so involved in work she'll forget to eat and the like. Brilliant on computers, yes. Brilliant when it comes to more common-sense issues, not so much. When I found her and Beast, he was half starved because she has no comprehension about how much a fella his size needs to eat."

"Why do you need my help?"

"You have my flash drive."

"Oh, come on, Jude. You and I both know you could take it from me if you really wanted." I pull it out of my purse and hand it over.

He takes the drive from me, slipping it in his pocket. Then he waves an airy hand. "I could use another person in this game. You know people in town. You can help me accomplish some of the tasks Grace has set for me. I'm an outsider. You have established connections I just don't have. And you're a reporter. We may need someone to tell the story when it's all said and done."

I snort. "I don't know what kind of townie power you think I have, but I can barely get people to tell me what their favorite ice cream flavor is."

"I think I can determine whether your helpfulness is worth the risk."

I bite my lip, thinking hard. This could be dangerous. Yes, it's a story. Yes, it could potentially save my job. Yes, it would mean not telling Fitz he's back to sleeping in his truck next month or Momma that her daughter is a big, fat failure. But is it worth getting involved? "I need to think about it."

He nods. "I would say take your time, but I get the sense it's running out."

"WILL you watch the front for me while I head to lunch?" Jane asks me.

"Sure."

It's not like I have a choice. No one is here except us. The guys have taken to disappearing at the same time every day because they can't handle taking over for the "secretary." It makes them feel like less than men when they don't know how to transfer calls coming in, even though it's like two buttons and the thing barely ever rings.

Besides, after the chat with Jude over burgers last night, I'm not doing much of anything except making a list of the pros and cons for getting involved with him.

I mean, getting involved with the whole Grace thing.

Pro: I could get the scoop of my life.

Con: I could end up in prison and become someone's bitch.

It's really a struggle to decide. I want more information and Jude dangled just enough to get me intrigued, the bastard. I can't help it.

After doing a bit of my own internet research, I've discovered some stuff about hackers and their lingo.

There are a few different types of hackers. There's white hat (the good guys), black hat (the bad guys with the malware and viruses and bank fraud), and something in between called grey hat (someone who maybe does this illegal stuff, but without malicious intent).

Jude mentioned script kiddies, which is apparently a term for hackers who just like to stream illegal movies and the like and don't really care much about being real hackers.

Then there are green hats (newbies trying to get into the hacking world) and red hats (vigilante types who fight against black hats instead of just reporting them).

If Jude is to be believed, Grace must be a red or grey hat.

And what is Jude?

I've got conflicting thoughts. My logical mind is screaming not to trust him while waving big red flags and calling me a dumbass. My vagina—the little slut—is doing her hair and makeup and wondering if I should get a wax just in case.

Not that he would take advantage of the goods even if I offered them up on a silver platter. Which I already did.

I've been trying not to think about that night, to shove it down with everything else in my life that makes me feel too much. But the memories fly out anyway, like a colony of bats escaping from the cave in my mind.

It was Begonia Day—the one day a year the entire BFU campus celebrates it's swine mascot with a giant party—and while the festivities on campus were over, Jude's house party was kicking off.

Jude and I were arguing, as usual. We had been having a disagreement as to whether pigs were monogamous—as we do—and he disappeared right when I was winning the argument because he had to "take care of some important business."

I figured he just had to help Beast settle down some belligerent guests or something, but after he'd been gone for over an hour, I went in search of him. If he thought he could walk away from a discussion I was winning, he had another think coming.

But he was nowhere to be found. The backyard was packed with people in pig masks drinking from the keg and dancing and talking.

The house was wall-to-wall people and stank like beer and too much cologne. He wasn't in the living room or playing cards in the kitchen or in the line for the bathroom.

So I meandered to the back of the house toward his room.

Pressing an ear to his door, I listened but couldn't hear anything but the thump of the party and shouts and laughter from down the hall.

I tried the door.

Locked.

Damn him, he had to be in there.

I knocked.

"Jude! I know you're in there. We weren't done with our discussion and you can't back out now," I yelled.

The door swung back and I opened my mouth, ready to tell him how pigs are not monogamous and only 3 to 6 percent of mammals are anyway, but when he opened the door, something was different.

He was still wearing that silly robe covered in cats that resembled Mr. Bojangles. He still had too much facial hair and needed a trim. I never liked long hair and beards on a guy, it just wasn't attractive. But he was wearing thick-framed black glasses. There they were, perched on the bridge of his nose.

I blinked. The nerd glasses lent a sense of refinement to his unkempt appearance. He was like a hipster without the affected flannel and PBR.

It was a stunning sort of contrast and it made him so, so . . . hot. It made *me* hot.

And that's when everything went off the rails. It was like my body took over my mind. I stepped through the doorway and grabbed his stupid, too-long hair and pressed my mouth against his bearded face.

His lips were softer than I imagined. The facial hair less scratchy and more . . . silky.

I must've shocked him because he didn't move for one long second, but then suddenly he was all fluid motion and sliding hands. Distantly, the door clicked shut behind me but I was too focused on his mouth on mine, his tongue sliding between my lips. My legs turned into jelly.

His confident hands made their way down my sides to my rear and then he lifted me and I wrapped my legs around him like we'd done this dance a million times before. I clung to his neck and he licked into my mouth like I was the best dessert he'd ever had. My body was on fire with need. More. I had to have more.

Needy noises slipped from my mouth without thought. He pulled his face back, though his hands held me against the hardest erection I'd ever felt, pressed directly into my center. I squirmed against him. Every cell in my body was on fire.

Then he turned with me still wrapped around him, and we moved over and down to his bed.

Yes.

This was what I wanted. But instead of coming over me and continuing our descent into wild, uninhibited passion, his kisses turned gentle. Soft. Less demanding and more . . . sweet.

Which wasn't bad either, but the sweet, gentle pecks and nips along my neck and back to my mouth turned into the longest, most frustrating make-out session of my life.

"I love this spot here," he said, his voice tickling my neck right before he kissed the sensitive spot behind my lobe. "You have the cutest freckles across the bridge of your nose," he murmured when his lips trailed over my cheek back to my mouth.

Between the compliments, we kissed. And the farthest we got was when I pulled off his shirt so I could kiss across his chest and ravish every bump and hard ridge, but he wouldn't let me go farther, though I attempted it.

And then we somehow fell asleep. And cuddled.

And he was a good snuggler, damn him to hell. I woke

up the next morning to find him wrapped around me, our hands mingling. He played with my fingers, sending shocks of awareness tingling up my arms. I wasn't naked from having a night of wild sex. Nope. I was in his boxers, ones with cats on them, and one of his T-shirts. Clothes he had kindly offered to make me more comfortable overnight.

For a few minutes, I savored the sensations. His heat at my back, his soft, rhythmic breathing, the smell of him on the sheets—the comforting scent of fresh linens combined with his citrusy aftershave.

He held me like I belonged there, his arms exuding possession and comfort, an intoxicating mix that made me instantly horny. And did he take advantage of me squirming against his giant erection?

No. No, he did not.

I turned and looked at him, and his cool blue eyes were like a hot tub on a snowy day—full of steam and comfort and warmth and sex.

But he didn't whisper dirty phrases in my ear. He didn't promise to make all my dreams come true. No. Instead, he whispered, "Can I take you to dinner later?"

And that's when it grabbed me. A heavy, squeezing vise around my rib cage, telling me to run.

And I did.

"Coffee," I said and rolled away from him.

I didn't really want coffee. My stomach was churning too much.

Maybe the real reason he didn't want to have sex with me was because he knew: I'm not worth the effort.

The little voice in my head was booming. And it was

telling me pain would be inevitable. It would be all too easy to fall for Jude, with his bedroom eyes and talented mouth and enough secrets to fill the Mississippi.

I reacted like I always do when people get too close. I ran. But the thing is . . . I don't want to run anymore.

The bell rings when someone pushes open the door at the *Daily Blue* office and I leap into work mode like I wasn't just fantasizing about hot bearded men.

"How can I help—" The question stalls out on my lips.

She's standing there, staring at me.

My palms sweat, my heart starts racing, my muscles tensing in a fight-or-flight response. No, it's not the creepy chick from *The Ring* climbing out of the well with her hair in her face. It's worse.

Taylor.

She's the epitome of the girl next door. Her dark hair is pulled back on one side with a flower clip. Her button-up shirt is happy and yellow. She's dressed like the kindergarten teacher she is, down to the paint stain on her cheek that should make her slovenly but instead is endearing.

Our eyes meet and she freezes and I know exactly what she's thinking, as clear as I can hear my own heartbeat. She wants to run. But that's never been Taylor's MO. It's mine.

It's not like I've been able to completely avoid seeing her at any point in the last four years; this town is way too small for that. But normally I'm more aware, and upon any kind of Chad or Taylor sighting, I hide. One time at the H-E-B I got stuck behind a stack of zucchini until they exited the premises. Not my most glorious twenty minutes, but it's better than being within breathing distance like I am now.

There's the brief moment where her eyes widen and she realizes it's me and then she marches right over and sets a piece of torn-out notebook paper on the counter.

"I'd like to place an announcement, please." Her voice is quiet but oh so familiar. It reminds me of late-night sleepovers, drinking pop on the front lawn, and zigzagging through the sprinklers on summer days when it was too hot to even think straight.

I wrench my eyes away from her and grab the paper. I can do this. Read the number of words, give her the price, and then she'll leave and this will all be over and I can go back to thinking about Jude and everything he told me and I can shove Taylor back into the cavern of things I don't like to think about.

My eyes run over the page.

It's a wedding announcement.

She's getting married. To Chad.

I swallow past the lump in my throat. I don't care. It doesn't matter.

Count the words on the announcement.

My eyes blur. Focus. I try three times and fail.

"That'll be thirty dollars." It's the best estimate I can muster even though it's at least ten over.

But she doesn't argue with me even though, knowing Taylor, she's already counted it out and made exact change.

She shuffles through her purse and I stare at the motivational poster on the wall that has been there since the last century. It's a picture of a rowing team at sunset with the word *TEAMWORK* spelled out in giant block letters underneath.

I count the number of oars in the water three times before she finally sets the bills on the counter, her fingers shaking slightly. "Annabel." Her voice is soft, but I don't let it sway the walls around my heart. "I'm so sorry about everything. So is Chad. I would really like to talk—"

"If that's all you needed?" I swipe the bills from the counter and turn my back to put the cash in the lockbox and make a record on the payment log.

"I— Won't you even listen to me?"

"I've got work to do." I busy myself shuffling papers around Jane's desk. I have nothing to do, but Taylor doesn't know that.

The bell jingles on the door as she leaves.

My head hangs forward.

That was the first time I've talked to Taylor in years. Not since . . . I push twelve more house-sized boulders down the memory shaft.

I knew things were serious with them. I couldn't avoid hearing about it, not in a town this small. Chad's father works with my friend Susie's brother at the manufacturing plant, and I've overheard the gossip from Cathy a time or two. Everyone thinks they're the cutest couple.

Chad is a newly hired cop—ironic, since Jude just mentioned his aversion to going to the cops, but Chad is the poster boy for angelic behavior and could never be involved in anything even slightly shady. He can't even tell white lies. And getting a job as a cop is not an easy feat in a town this small, since you basically have to wait for someone to die or retire for there to be an opening. Blue

Falls isn't exactly a hotbed of murder and crime. Being a police officer has been his dream ever since we were kids and playing cops and robbers in Taylor's basement.

And then there's Taylor. She's teaching kindergarten at the elementary school.

They're like the lamest, most boring Hallmark Channel movie ever come to life. At least, that's the lie I tell myself.

An image flickers in my mind, the long-suppressed memory surfacing like an old-timey movie: Chad's face when I told him all my embarrassing truths, when I put myself out there and he crushed me with one sympathetic look and a few honest words. Honesty that cut through a load of lies being fed to me by someone who was my best friend. Or so I thought. The old, familiar humiliation rises like a fast-moving tide up my chest, threatening to drown me, but I shove it back down, back into the cave in my mind where I put everything that hurts me.

It doesn't matter. I'm going to do something with my life, leave this town. And I don't need anyone else to do that.

Except . . . I glance down at my pro and con list again.

I still need to keep my day job.

Chapter Six

Friendship is constant in all other things.
—William Shakespeare, *Much Ado About Nothing*

Annabel

"HOLD ON. Who is Taylor? Why haven't I ever heard of her? Do you really need that much whiskey?"

"An old friend, I don't talk about it, and yes I really do." I take another shot and tap the glass on the bar twice, motioning the bartender for another.

It's girls' night. Reese wanted to go to Granny's to test out the new archery set, but I drove us here instead. Bodean's. The only good place in town to go when you want to get trashed. I mean, Granny's got moonshine, it's true, but getting drunk and playing with pointy things seemed like a bad decision.

Bodean's is your typical small-town country bar. The interior is smothered in dark wood. There's a large dance floor sticky with cheap booze. A variety of colorful, fraying posters are tacked up behind the bar. It's patronized by everyone from city employees enjoying a beer after work to farmers to college students. Even though it's somewhat early, people are already trickling in through the front door and filling the sparse seating behind us.

"So why aren't you and Taylor friends anymore? What happened?"

"I might lose my job," I tell Reese instead of answering her question. I'm not drunk enough to share that piece of my past, although I know I'll get there quick. Despite the way I'm mainlining Tennessee whiskey tonight, I'm not usually a big drinker and it doesn't take much.

She grimaces.

"I suck at writing."

"You don't suck."

"I just . . . need something better to write about. Something interesting. Something that will wow my boss and let me keep my job. Otherwise Fitz and I might be moving in with you."

The bartender sets down another shot and I ask for a beer to chase it with.

She wrinkles her nose. "My room at Jude's is barely big enough for me."

"I know. Which is why I need some ideas so Fitz doesn't have to sleep on the street."

Reese thinks for a moment. This is one of the things I love about Reese. She never jumps to conclusions or judgments. She thinks and offers solutions. "When I'm stuck, I like to make a list."

"Yeah, I do that, too," I murmur, eyeballing the next shot, thinking about my pro and con list about Jude. I down the shot. "What do you think about Jude?"

Reese wrinkles her nose and takes a small sip of her beer. "In what context?"

I wave a hand. "In general. You seem to trust him. Thank you," I tell the bartender as he sets my beer down. He nods and whisks away the empty shot glasses.

"He hasn't given me any reason to not trust him."

"You're so logical."

"Is that a bad thing?"

"I guess not."

Reese taps a finger on the bar. "He's a good landlord. And roommate. Very clean. He knows a lot of things, too."

"What do you mean?"

"I mean, if it weren't for him, I might not have come up with my idea for the school."

Reese is next-level smart, but she was having trouble early in the term picking her major and running out of time to decide. She finally settled on a dual major and came up with plans to eventually open a school in Blue Falls for people like her—i.e., super smart people who lack social skills.

Okay, so I made the last part up, but she is planning on opening a school for the gifted and talented.

"What did Jude have to do with it?" I ask.

"He introduced me to Fynn."

"Who the heck is Fynn?"

"He's Jude's Little Brother. Not literally, but you know, Jude does the whole Big Brother thing."

"Wait. What?" When the hell does he have time for that in between his other nefarious activities?

Reese nods. "Fynn is his little. Fynn's very advanced for his age and I've been helping him obtain access to information and resources that aren't available at the local elementary." She taps her chin. "A month ago or so I had a cancellation for a class, and when I went home, Jude was heading out to meet Fynn and asked me for a ride. After spending time with Fynn, I came up with the idea for the school. Blue Falls doesn't have anything for gifted kids, and they need support and encouragement. It was like Jude knew what I needed before I did. And what Fynn needed, come to think of it. Yet it was seemingly coincidental."

"Ugh, that's just like him." I drink some of my beer.

When I put the glass down, Reese is watching me. "What is going on between you two?"

"Why do you look so tired lately?" I counter.

Reese is so easy to get off track.

She grimaces. "I haven't been sleeping much. School is a lot of work, and then when I stay the night with Fitz—"

"Wait. Stop there." I hold up a hand. "No, I don't want to hear about your sleepless nights with my brother."

"Then tell me why you're avoiding my question about Jude."

"Why do moths like light?"

Her whole face brightens. "They actually don't, it's a behavior called transverse orientation . . . Wait a minute."

She opens her mouth to call me out, but before she can speak, someone steps up to the bar in between us.

"Good evening, Annabel."

"Hey, Rudy," I say. Probably the only time I've been relieved to see him, since it's saving me from a conversation about Jude and myself. However, it doesn't bode well that he stepped between Reese and I and we're sitting at the bar with no graceful way to exit the conversation.

Let the vortex of conversation begin.

"Who's your friend? I don't believe we've met."

He's eyeing Reese like she's a steak dinner.

"This is Fitz's girlfriend, Reese. Reese, this is Rudy."

"Pleased to meet you," Reese says formally, putting out her hand.

Rudy shakes it but he's already deflating. Mission accomplished. "May I purchase either one of you a drink?"

"That's mighty kind of you, but we're still working on the ones we have." I motion to Reese's mostly full beer and my own, which I've only taken a few sips from.

"Are y'all coming to the charity Turkey Trot on Saturday?" He nods to one of the flyers behind the bar pimping the annual charity event dance-off.

"Hadn't intended on it," I say.

"I'm not much of a dancer," Reese says.

"I have to go to the bathroom."

So, maybe I'm not that great of a friend since I'm bailing, but Reese is terrible at conversation. If anyone can get rid of Rudy, it's her. I try to message her with my eyes as I run off. It must work, because I pee and lollygag and wash my hands three times, and when I get back,

Rudy is in the corner of the bar talking to a bachelorette party. They must've come in while I was taking my sweet-ass time.

"Thank God you got rid of him."

"He likes to chat," Reese acknowledges. "Ask him for the time and he'll tell you how to build a watch."

"How did you accomplish the Herculean feat of making him go away?"

"I started talking about string theory and singularities and then the group with the penis crowns came in and did the rest of the work for me." She nods over at the party.

I laugh.

"Are you ready to talk about Taylor yet?"

"Nope."

"I saved you. You owe me."

"I owe you jack shit."

"Then let's talk about Jude and how y'all are meant to be together." She bats her eyes like a love-struck loon and I want to strangle her.

"You're gonna make us fail the Bechdel test."

"Well, you don't want to talk about work, and you don't wanna talk about Taylor, so I have limited options. You gotta let stuff out sometimes, Annabel."

"I got nothing to say about Jude. It's lust. A biochemical reaction because I like his pheromones."

Reese tilts her head. "If you're going to use a scientific explanation for your lack of belief in love and romance, then I would like to point out that, biologically, it's advantageous for females to have a monogamous relationship due to the length of time it takes to produce and equip offspring with the necessary skills for survival."

I groan and slap my forehead. "I'm not arguing about this with you."

"That's probably wise. So we don't fail Bechdel, tell me about Taylor."

I stare at her.

She stares back, blank faced.

I take a long drink of the tepid beer in front of me. I'm going to need it even to reveal a smidge of this.

"Taylor and I were best friends when we were kids. Well, there were three of us who were all besties. Taylor, Chad, and myself."

"What happened?"

"What happened is . . ." I rub the back of my neck. "We're not friends anymore. But I keep running into her, and today I couldn't run away and hide like I normally do."

Reese gasps. "I'm the one who hides in bushes, not you. You're supposed to be the strong one."

"Well guess what, buttercup? I hate to shatter your worldview, but you aren't the only geek in this friendship. I'm a total weirdo. I just try to hide it more than you."

"I've discovered it's better off to own your weird."

I snort.

"So why couldn't you run and hide today?"

"Taylor came in to drop off an announcement at the paper and I was covering the front desk. She's marrying Chad."

"And this bothers you because . . ."

"I don't want Chad, if that's what you're thinking."

"I wasn't thinking anything."

I take another drink, trying to wait out Reese, but she's

not talking and she's staring at me like a creep, waiting for me to continue. I sigh and give in. A little. "It bothers me because . . . it's hard to see her. Since we aren't friends anymore."

"And you don't want to tell me why that is?"

I decide to go for minimal words, maximum impact. "She lied to me."

"Ah. 'It is easier to forgive an enemy than to forgive a friend.' "

"Feels true."

"William Blake." She takes a sip of her beer and then puts a hand on my shoulder. "I won't ask you for details if you don't want to disclose them, but I do want you to know I'm here for you if you ever change your mind."

I lean into her. "You're so nice. And smart. I can see why Fitz loves you. Thanks, Reesey-poo."

"I can see the liquor is starting to kick in." She stares at her own beer. "I think mine is, too. The lack of sleep is making me a lightweight."

I sit up suddenly, and she must be right because the room spins a smidge before righting itself again. "We should dance."

"There's no music. I'm a terrible dancer. But sure."

I grin. She's such a pushover. "You're a good friend, Reese."

She straightens, a smile growing on her face. "I am? I mean, I am. You're my only friend, so there is that."

A few hours later, we've danced with each other and the bachelorette party—but not Rudy. I switch from beer to water but Reese does not.

She can normally drink jars of moonshine without

getting buzzed, so the lack of sleep must really be affecting her. By ten o'clock I have to walk slash carry her home, listening to her talk about Fitz almost the whole time and how much she misses him.

"You saw him this morning."

"It's been so long!"

Once we make it to Jude's, the house is surprisingly quiet and empty. "No party tonight?"

"Jude's been real busy. We haven't been having as many fancy shindigs as we used to."

"What's he been busy with?" Does she know anything about what he's involved in?

But she just shrugs. "I dunno."

Beast is in the living room alone, watching a movie. No sign of Jude.

I help Reese put on a clean shirt and put her to bed.

"Tell Fitz I love him." She collapses face-first onto the mattress.

"Tell him yourself, weirdo," I murmur before tucking her in and shutting her door behind me.

By myself in the quiet hallway, I stop to listen. The muted sound of voices from the TV echoes down the hall. I glance in the opposite direction, down the darkened corridor, toward Jude's bedroom.

I should go home, but my feet carry me to the back.

Light emanates from under the doorframe.

I knock.

He takes so long, I almost leave. Half of me doesn't want him to answer and the other half wants it a little too much, and not only because I don't wanna be a pathetic loser.

The door swings open. He's wearing jeans slung low on his hips, and a plain white T-shirt hugs his chest. I remember that chest. Tan skin stretched over firm muscle. My eyes lift to his face and I swallow.

Glasses.

He's wearing the damn glasses again.

My heart stutters and my stomach flips, but my voice is thankfully strong. "I'm in."

Chapter Seven

It is a great misfortune to be alone, my friends; and it must be believed that solitude can quickly destroy reason.
—Jules Verne, *The Mysterious Island*

Jude

WHEN I OPEN the bedroom door to find Annabel outside it, I'm equal parts elated and cautious.

There's something in her eyes, a frazzled, hyper look she tends to get that screams to tread softly.

"Come in, then."

She moves past me and I shut the door behind her as she walks into the center of the room, glancing around, her eyes lingering on the bed where Mr. Bojangles is sleeping near my pillow.

Is she thinking about the last time she was in here? I hope she is. I've thought about it nearly every day.

She sits next to Mr. Bojangles, dropping her purse on the floor. Her eyes meet mine.

"So. Tell me a story." She pets my furry, white feline. He stretches his limbs out on a yawn, and his purring fills the space between us.

I push away from the door and amble toward her. "I suppose I should start with Grace's little project, because that seems to be the source of the issue. She was working on an interesting program. She created software capable of detecting data breaches and tracing their source."

"Don't they already have stuff like that?"

I sit next to her on the bed, a couple feet away. "Similar. Not the same. Grace's program can catch even the sneakiest breaks in a firewall and then it does something unique. It attaches itself to the intruder and works back to find the source—no matter how many different IPs and channels they're moving through. It also snapshots information and secures it in case of ransomware attacks. She'd been running unauthorized tests on it, infiltrating governmental databases."

"So you think, what, something about this program led her here?"

"I'm not sure. A week after she left, we received an encrypted message, coordinates to Blue Falls. Specifically, the university."

Her head tilts. "That's why you run all these . . . extracurricular activities for people from BFU. You're trying to get intel."

"Partially. There was a reason she sent me those coordinates, along with a request to follow the money trail.

Someone is funneling significant funds through the university. I just don't know who or why. Running the games is also a way to make money, too. It's enabled me to enroll Beast in higher education, which he's never had the opportunity to pursue. It is also a way to ingratiate myself with a section of the community that may be involved in what Grace is chasing, and connections are never a bad thing to have."

"So you have no idea what Grace is doing other than it could be connected to this program she was developing?"

"I've been trying to get my own intel, but it's challenging. Grace typically requests simple things, like leaving her money in places she can access later. I do think the dark vans may be involved as well."

"Who do you think is in the vans?"

I rub my beard. "If I had to guess, FBI."

"Really?"

"It fits their general MO. Except they normally have logos on their vans to make them blend. Someone has been retasking satellites for local coverage, too, which only those working for a government agency could do."

"Why would someone in Blue Falls want Grace's program? And why would the FBI be here, too?"

I tap my lips in thought. "The University has the best CS department this side of Texas. It's not out of the question that someone attending or teaching could be involved. Someone either found what Grace was working on and is trying to replicate it, or they stole it and she followed them here. Her software would be useful for a variety of reasons. They could sell it themselves, or they could use it to eliminate their competition."

She rubs Mr. Bojangles's head with gentle fingers. "This could be a heavy story."

"I know."

"Can I ask you a more personal question?"

I meet her eyes. "Of course."

"Beast and Grace are brother and sister. How do you fit in? Why are you helping them?"

"It's hard to explain. We're not blood, but we may as well be."

She watches me, waiting for me to continue.

Maybe I should tell her everything. My whole story. I know she's curious. She's attempted to weasel it out of me many times in the past. Some innate intuition tells me it would be helpful to reveal my own shameful past, to show her she's safe to share her own when she's ready. Because Annabel has more defenses than Area 51.

"To really understand everything, I have to tell you about my past."

"I won't put your personal story out for print. No one would give a shit anyway," she jokes with a small smile.

I lean forward, resting my elbows on my knees. "I originally hail from Valdosta. That's where my family is. My parents were . . . It's difficult to find adequate phrases to aptly describe them. They were very religious. Not the *love your neighbors and go to church on Sundays* type, but the *Harry Potter is the creation of Satan* type. To them, going to church daily and praying for hours while flogging yourself is barely enough to make up for the unending sins of humanity."

"Wait." She lifts a hand. "I'm sorry, Harry Potter?"

I shrug. "Witchcraft."

Her eyes widen. "Oh."

"Oh. Yes. I had to sneak around to pursue my interests in computers and technology. Luckily, I made a few friends at the library, kind librarians and volunteers who would help me and let me work on the computers past the time limits and sometimes even after closing.

"I spent a lot of time teaching myself. I quickly developed a keen interest in gaming and software. But I still could not pursue such types of recreational activities at home. My parents were quite convinced technology would be the downfall of our society."

"They might not be wrong."

"Maybe not, but it wasn't a mild distaste for smartphones that compelled them, but the power of religious fervor. They were beyond anything that could be imagined. More than fanatical. It's hard to explain, but it wasn't normal. It was more comparable to a cult. We had no TV, no radios, no links to anything outside the church. There were no holidays. No birthday celebrations or gifts or anything that could lead to gluttony or greed or any kind of deadly sin. Any mention of such things made them very . . . angry."

As if sensing my distress, Mr. Bojangles pads over to me, settling himself into my lap. I rub his head and continue the tale.

"The library is where I met Grace. Of course I noticed Beast first. He was large even as a young teen. They were always together."

"He's hard to miss."

I nod. "I didn't have friends. I wasn't sent to school, because they take the Lord out of the classroom—even at parochial schools—too much for my parents' liking. Beast and Grace were always there at the same time I was, and Grace was on the computers a lot. Beast was formidable, and I avoided them initially. But then I noticed things. They took care of each other. He would look after her, scare off anyone who tried to get near her, even made her take breaks for food and water. He was always protecting her. You wouldn't know they were related. Grace is tiny and blonde and resembles a frail pixie. She wasn't more than seven or eight at the time.

"I became a bit fascinated with them, actually. Who they were. Where they came from. I was jealous of their bond because I had no one. I was all alone in the world. I often found reasons to lurk nearby. Quite creepy, really."

Annabel smiles but doesn't respond. She's listening, leaning toward me. She pets Mr. Bojangles on my lap.

"Then one day, I was walking behind Grace and I caught a glimpse of what was on her screen. It was a scanning algorithm searching for open shares. When I confronted her about it, to my surprise, she told me exactly what she was doing and then let me watch her finish opening a backdoor to infiltrate."

I hadn't realized: she'd been paying attention to me, too. I was shocked at what she was willing to share. It was not what I had anticipated.

"It was a story that had been on the news. Some black hat had hacked into a nonprofit, no-kill cat shelter. They had recently completed a big fundraiser and the hackers took every last dime. Grace tracked them like it was nothing. She returned the money, then sent the proof and location of the bad guys to the authorities. Anonymously, of course. Then she asked if I wanted to work with her. And I did."

"That's crazy."

"It was. It's also how I got Mr. Bojangles."

We both look down at him.

She scratches his little white head and his eyes fall shut in ecstasy. "So you guys just, what, lived together after that?"

"Not right away. Grace and Beast were already living on their own. Their parents were deceased. They wanted to put Beast in a facility. Grace couldn't let that happen. She was stealing money for their support, but only from black hats and only when she couldn't return it to the original source. It was barely enough for them to live in a crap apartment and have enough for basic life necessities. She felt that justified the illegal behavior."

"But you didn't?"

I shrug. "It wasn't my place to judge. She needed money to live. And she was merely a child, but I wanted to help them."

"Grey moral area."

"Exactly. It's not as though I hadn't done the same." I watch her closely. "When I was a younger person, before I became acquainted with technology, I had my own habit of stealing."

"Stealing what? Like loaves of bread?" She smiles.

"It does sound rather *Oliver Twist* in nature, but I was a pickpocket. Wallets. Smartphones. It was easy. I always excelled at sleight of hand and magic tricks. It's how I got enough money to purchase my own computer, and then once I had that," I shrug, "I moved on to more ethical ventures with my technological skills. But I couldn't possibly begrudge Grace for doing what she needed when I had done much the same. For me it was also a way to control something when the rest of my life felt so out of control."

Annabel nods. She doesn't appear appalled by my past behavior, so I continue.

"As soon as I made enough to contribute, I left home. Grace and Beast came with me. I was seventeen, old enough that the fake ID I made could pass as legitimate." The memory of fleeing one sunny afternoon assails me. It was sunset. I had only a hint of a plan and enough money in my pocket to get us out of town.

"Didn't your parents send, like, the cops after you or something?"

"I would be surprised if they spent any significant amount of time or energy searching."

She frowns. "Why?"

"After I was born, Momma couldn't have any more kids."

"So?"

I shrug. "So they kind of . . . blamed me for that."

"How is that your fault?"

"It's not, but that's not how they see it. I ruined her ability to serve the Lord as a woman was meant to."

Annabel snorts. "You've got to be kidding me."

" 'Procreation is the Lord's plan,' " I recite. "Women are here to bear children and then rear them. That's their sole purpose."

Annabel's face is sufficiently horrified. "I wouldn't last five minutes."

I grin. "It's one of the things I appreciate about you. And one of the reasons I love a good romance movie. I wasn't allowed to watch any movies, let alone romantic ones. Full of sin. They set a bad tone as well, because romance isn't necessary when women are only good for one thing." I lift my brows at her in challenge and take a moment to let her stew on that.

"So you guys have been living together this whole time . . . and then . . ."

"And then Grace disappeared and started sending me messages from Blue Falls. You have to understand, Grace is like a sister to me. She and Beast are the only family I have."

I may have helped them in some ways, but the truth is, they saved me.

"I wasn't completely brainwashed by my parents' upbringing, but living my life in an environment where I was unsafe to be myself, to share my hopes and dreams . . ."

It made me hard. Cold. Closed off. Grace and Beast showed me there was another way. That there were people who would care about me enough so I could be myself without fear.

"With Grace and Beast, it was the first time I experienced true family. True empathy. They cared for me not despite my shame and past behavior, but because of it."

Annabel swallows and glances away.

Maybe I've pushed too far. Given too much. I can't say I regret my past, though. It helped make me who I am today. I learned how to read people because I had to. I knew to stop talking whenever my mother's lips thinned. I knew to leave the room when my father's right eyebrow started to tic, and to flee the house altogether if that tic turned into a squinty-eyed glare. It was the only way to survive unscathed.

"What was on the flash drive you got at the middle school? That was something from Grace?"

"Yes. It's spyware. The link to a software download along with the name of a person."

"She wants you to spy on someone?"

"She wants me to plant spyware on a particular person's cell phone. This is precisely the type of task I could use assistance with. While Beast is a good distraction in some ways, he doesn't speak and he tends to incite fear more than anything else."

"Have you had to plant spyware on other people before?" Her eyes are bright with interest.

"Only a couple of people who frequent my social events, people who appeared to have money funneling through their accounts. But those ended up being dead ends. Hopefully this one won't be as well, but there's only one way to know."

She nods. "Who's the mark?"

"Bryce Butler. You know him?"

She shrugs. "Name sounds vaguely familiar. How do we install the spyware?"

She said "we." That's a positive indication. "It's fairly easy, actually. It's what we like to call an evil maid attack. We simply need to get our hands on his phone for a minute. There's a secure site set up to download the software. It takes less than thirty seconds to install, wipes its own tracks, and then we'll be able to access everything on his phone and use it as a listening device."

"And I presume Grace will also somehow have access to this information?"

"Likely."

"What would my job be in all this?"

"We have the same goal, to get ahold of Bryce's phone for a couple minutes and download the spyware. Between the two of us, we can find an opportunity. It could be as simple as asking to use his phone to call someone or sneaking it out of his pocket."

She blinks down at Mr. Bojangles and then clasps her hands in her lap, thinking. "When are we doing this?"

"You free Wednesday?"

"I can be."

I nod. "Every Wednesday Bryce goes to the same place, some kind of gathering in the basement of the library."

She frowns. "They don't have any functions at the library on Wednesday nights. I've covered the calendar of events before."

I shrug and rub at my beard. "I suppose it's a meeting, of sorts."

"What, like an AA meeting?"

Should I tell her? It might be more fun if she figures it out on her own. "Not exactly."

"Well, what is it?"

"You know, I'm not entirely sure. It's some kinda group meeting, but they're a bit reticent. I know where and when and that Bryce will be there. You said you were in. Did you mean it?"

She watches me for a moment, brown eyes soft in the dim light. Then her shoulders straighten and she nods. "I'll be there."

Chapter Eight

No man, for any considerable period, can wear one face to himself and another to the multitude, without finally getting bewildered as to which may be the true.

—Nathaniel Hawthorne, *The Scarlet Letter*

Annabel

I PICK Jude up Wednesday night before the "meeting," whatever that means, honking for him from the driveway.

My head is still spinning with all of the information he unloaded.

How much he shared of himself, all of his past. How much he's been through . . . it's astounding. And the way he put it out there, he made it seem so easy. Like it's no big deal. A secret part of me wishes I could live like that but life has proven that every time I open up my heart, it gets ripped to shreds. Every time. Whether it's my writing, my friends, or even my own momma.

After a few minutes, Jude saunters out of the house carrying two brown paper bags, one in each hand.

He motions for me to pop the trunk and sets whatever he has in the back.

He slides into the passenger seat of my small Honda Civic, shutting us into the small space together.

"Good evening, Annabel." His voice is low and slow.

I ignore the tingles shooting down my spine at the way he says my name. "Hey Jude." I laugh. "Ha ha, get it? 'Hey Jude'?"

"Mighty original of you," he deadpans.

He's dressed simply, jeans and a black T-shirt. His presence damn near fills up the whole car along with the scent of his cologne—a faint smell mixed with soap and man and citrus. Basically, he smells like something I want to roll around in and lick. "You're looking mighty fine tonight," he says.

I'm dressed somewhat provocatively in tight jeans, tight shirt, extra makeup. "This is what you do when you're trying to be a distraction and get access to some guy's phone." I pull out of his driveway and head down the street in the direction of the library.

"You might find those efforts are fruitless."

"Why's that?" I glance over at him in the passenger seat and he gives me a slow smile and says nothing.

"Did you find out anything more about what this whole meeting is about?" I already asked around at work and checked the community calendar again, but there's nothing.

"It's possible."

"Why don't you tell me?"

"You'll find out soon enough."

He's right, because the library is only a few miles down the road. In less than ten minutes, we're parking.

He jumps out first, grabbing the bags from the trunk.

I meet him at the back of the car and he hands over one of the sacks. "Here. You're gonna need this."

"What is it?" I can't tell what it is on the surface, but it feels soft and fuzzy. Maybe some kind of blanket or something? Maybe it's a movie night and he brought me something to sit on. I reach in to pull it out but he tugs on my arm.

"No time. Come on, we're late."

I follow him down the side of the building to a set of stairs that head down to the basement. We stop in front of a large metal double door. He knocks twice and there's a responding knock on the other side. Three sharp raps.

Jude counters with one, then a pause, then three more, and the door swings open.

This is so weird. What is happening here? This is more than a movie night.

A woman close to my age, probably midtwenties, is on the other side. She's cute, small, blonde, and blue eyed and has a wide smile. "Welcome." Her head tilts. "I haven't seen y'all here before."

"It's our first time." Jude grins at her—as he does—and she blinks at him, straightening up and pushing out her chest a little bit more. He sticks out a hand. "I'm Jude Parker."

So I guess we're not going incognito here. Alrighty then.

"It's a pleasure to meet you. I'm Rachel." She shakes his hand and then turns to me.

"Annabel."

"Everyone is in the reading room at the end of the hall, on the right," she says after shaking my hand, too. "You can get dressed in the closet—it's a walk-in, everyone leaves their bags in there—or use the bathroom if you prefer. It's just over here." She points to a door. "The band is playing in about a half hour, and there's some snacks at the back of the room. Eat as much as you like! Some people like to keep in character the whole time and won't eat the people food." She grins at us.

I am so confused, but I try to hide it by nodding and smiling. In character? Is this some kind of acting thing?

"Thank you kindly," Jude says, ushering me down the hall.

"What does she mean, in character? And we're getting dressed into what, exactly?" I peer inside the bag again but I still can't compute.

We go into the reading room and it's full of people.

People in suits.

Not nice, three-piece suits or competent pantsuits. Oh no, they are all dressed in costumes. And I realize exactly what this is. Furries. Some are in full-body costumes, some in only tails and ears and paw-covered feet.

I don't know what to do. Or what to say. There's a giant teddy bear with a tie talking to a grey cat in a tutu. A group of wolves of various colors—brown and green and blue—sits in a circle in the corner. Another girl is wearing bunny ears and she's drinking coffee and talking to a guy with a horse's tail. There's also a unicorn and a zebra setting up instruments in the corner.

What the actual fuck?

I don't realize I'm staring, open mouthed, slack jawed, until Jude tugs me into the closet, and shuts the door. Everything disappears from my eyesight except Jude.

"Here." He reaches into the bag I'm holding and pulls out a soft brown costume.

He grins, handing me the brown material and I hold it up in a daze.

"The head is still in the bag," he says.

His phrasing gives me pause. "That's not what I want to hear right now. It sounds as if you're discussing a body part."

He laughs. "You don't have to wear it if you don't want to, but I think you might rather enjoy it." He shoves one leg into his suit.

His suit has white fur. If he's dressing like Mr. Bojangles, I might die. Or murder him. His head will be the one in the bag.

"Jude," I hiss at him. "What the fresh hell is this?"

"It's a furry event."

"A what?"

"You know, people who dress up in animal costumes. They hang out, create art, play music, and such." He hikes the suit up so his legs are covered up to his waist.

I'm silent for about three seconds watching him pull on the furry white costume. "You brought me into a stuffed-animal orgy?"

Now he's laughing silently, shoulders shaking. "It's not

an orgy, but I like how you think. It would be most difficult to penetrate, I imagine."

"This isn't funny!"

He stands up and grins at me. "You're right, it's not funny. And it's not what you think. It's not weird or sexual. They're just people getting together like anyone else. Don't pass judgment until you've tried it for yourself."

"Okay, fine, but don't you think you could have mentioned this, I don't know, yesterday?"

Now he laughs out loud, the prick. "I'm helping you. You're gonna have to learn to deal with the unexpected if you want to be a writer. Think about it this way, you're undercover. Just go with it. Oh, and I may have told Rachel that you're a reporter and you want to write about the positive aspects of furry culture to help contradict negative portrayals from the mainstream media." And with that little kicker and a final panty-melting grin, he yanks the bodysuit up and slides in his arms. The costume has a bright pink shirt.

He pulls a head out of his bag. It is a Mr. Bojangles outfit.

I press my lips together. "I can't take you seriously like this."

"Sounds like a you problem."

"How are we gonna find Bryce? And get his phone when we're wandering around in these, these, full-body costumes?"

"Well, you see, the paws on the hands are removable."

I lift a brow.

He chuckles and pulls out his phone, pushing some keys, and then holding the phone to his ear.

"Hear anything?"

I strain to listen but all I hear is talking from outside this room. "No."

"Then he's got it on him, most likely."

"What if he doesn't? What if he left it at home? What if it's in here but turned off?"

He cocks his head at me. "You worry too much. It will work out."

"What if it doesn't?"

He shrugs and turns away. "Then we move on to plan B."

"We don't even have a plan A!"

"Sure we do. First, we find Bryce. Then we get his phone." He shrugs. "We'll figure it out. Improvise. These things always have a way of working out."

"Ugh." I yank my costume out of the bag. It's a brown mouse with a wide smile and cheerful green eyes.

I stare down at the mouse head in my hands.

"You couldn't have gotten me one with just tails or something?"

"I'll have you know this is a very lush and expensive suit and I picked it out specifically for you to show we're serious here. We need to go all out and all in."

He pulls the headwear on. The Mr. Bojangles face is rather bitchy looking. Suits him. He smacks me on the shoulder and says, "See you out there." And he marches into the room full of furry people like this is no big deal and hey what else is there to do on a Wednesday night?

"Screw it," I whisper and get dressed. If he can do it, I can do it. I can be chill. I can go with the flow. I'm breezy.

I take my time getting dressed and then a few deep

breaths before I tug the head on. The mouth and eyes create holes big enough to see and breathe through, so at least I don't feel like I'm being going to hyperventilate.

And actually, having my whole body and face covered is kind of . . . nice. Like I'm hiding. No one will know who I am under all this. Nothing to be ashamed of.

The band starts up and I walk out into the room. The music isn't half bad, actually, a cover of a Taylor Swift song.

I glance around, trying to spot Jude's pink shirt.

Some people are dancing in the open space in front of the band, while others congregate near the food table. It's hard to see my periphery because I only have the eyeholes in front.

Someone walks up and stops next to me. A bright green turtle. She's got the furry outfit and shell on her back but no headpiece. It's the woman from the front door, Rachel.

"Hey! Y'all having fun?"

"Sure."

"Jude told me you wanted to talk about furry stuff."

"Yeah, of course." Maybe this will make an interesting article, but I really can't imagine Bruce's response during the pitch meeting. Probably something along the lines of, *That's nuttier than a five-pound fruitcake!*

Rachel tilts her head at me. "Are you really uncomfortable?"

"Is it that obvious?"

"Even your mask looks like it's constipated."

Surprised, I laugh. "I'm just not used to wearing . . . this."

She grins. "It's okay if you aren't comfortable in the headpiece, you can take it off. It can get hot in there anyway, and it's harder to have a conversation."

I pull the mouse head off and hold it in front of me. I blink at the sudden openness.

"Let me break it down for you a little. There are no rules here. Some furries don't talk at all while in costume, they just mime. That's the great part, you get to choose. You should do whatever makes you comfortable. Some people like the headpieces, some don't." She shrugs. "Depends on the fursona."

"Fursona?"

Her brows lift. "Your boyfriend mentioned you wanted to write an article. I thought you would have more background info before you came."

We both look over at him. He's holding both arms out and saying, "Babies!"

"He's not my boyfriend. We're just friends."

Her eyes skitter over Jude's pink and white form. He is not hot in that costume. Well, maybe he is. It's not really his looks, it's his whole . . . aura. He's over by the band, doing the running man while furries clap and cheer him on. They even start chanting his name.

How does he do it? We literally just got here.

"Is that right?" she asks. "He single?"

Something constricts in my stomach. "I mean, not yet. We're friends, technically, but you know, it's heading in that direction." The words pop out without thought and I thank the lord Jude can't hear me from across the room. I would die of embarrassment and he would never let me live it down if he knew I was . . . what, jealous? No, it's not that. It can't be that. I'm just protecting him from, uh, untoward advances.

Rachel tsks and shakes her head. "Well, too bad then. But good on you, girl! Anyway, let me tell you more about fursonas. You want a drink?"

I glance around, but I'm not entirely sure what Bryce looks like, let alone how to pick him out amid the furry crowd. I guess I'll leave it up to Jude and do what he asked. Blend. Improvise. "Sure." I follow her over to the snack table. "I did do some research. Enough to know that furries aren't all about orgies, like some people might think." I roll my eyes at *those* people. Those people I might have been one of five minutes ago.

Rachel smiles. "That's true. Totally a misconception and a stereotype perpetuated by the media to sensationalize something they don't understand. We have sex just as much as anyone else. Mostly we like to get together and dress up. A lot of us like to share our furry-themed artwork and crafts related to the fandom. Wanna see?"

Over at one of the tables, they've got a setup of artwork. There are actually some really good sketches and paintings and even comic books.

"So if it's not about sex, then why all the secrecy for the meeting?"

"Because people don't understand. They assume we're all a bunch of weirdos, but it's okay for them to geek out over *Game of Thrones* and the Super Bowl. It's about meeting up with like-minded people and feeling . . . seen."

A smidge of guilt flickers in my chest about my initial reaction. I put a hand on her arm. "I promise to keep names and everything confidential."

Her responding smile is bright and sincere. "Thanks. I appreciate that."

Rachel continues to fill me in on furry culture while others come over periodically and talk to her and hug her and some are introduced to me. I kinda see what Rachel means. Everyone is so happy and kind and accepting.

Eventually, I put the mask back on, mostly because I'm sick of holding it and also I have no idea where to put it. Besides, once I'm covered completely, I'm more relaxed. And I think there's something in the juice because the room is a little tipsy.

After a spell, Jude walks over with a black and white tabby.

"Hey, Annabel, this is Bryce. I was informing him that it's our first time and you were a little nervous."

I nod and we shake hands.

Rachel immediately turns her attention to Jude, yapping his ear off and putting her furry hand on his furry arm, the tramp.

But that leaves me to talk to . . . Bryce. Of course Jude found him.

We stand by the food table and I have no idea what to say to get some guy to give me his phone.

May as well start with a compliment. "I like your"—I wave a hand—"cat. It's very . . . nice."

Jesus, has anyone ever sucked at espionage as much as I do?

"I like your mouse, too," he says.

"Thanks. Hey, you're a cat and I'm a mouse." I force a laugh. "It's like we're . . . Tom and Jerry."

I'm not funny. But he, kindly, laughs at my terrible

joke, then almost as an aside mentions, "I could chase you, if you're into it."

Uhhhhh . . . "Ha, ha, ha." Okay, so he's also not funny, but then . . . I can't tell because with the mask, all I can see is a cat with shiny eyes and a furry face tilted in my direction. Is he serious?

"So you want to? We could go outside?" he says into my silence.

"Um." Holy shit, he really wants to chase me around in our costumes. Like we're really doing this.

And can I say no? Should I say no? I can't say no. I need his phone. I need him to ask for my number or do something so I can find out if his phone is on him without straight up asking.

"Sure, fine." My big head nods and then yes, I'm following him outside.

I'm going outside with a strange man so we can chase each other around the front lawn of the library at ten o'clock at night.

Well, I guess this is more exciting than listening to Reese and Fitz get it on.

We go outside, walking the whole way in complete silence while I internally debate every life choice that has led me to this moment. Once we're outside, in the dark, Bryce does a little leap and lifts his hands like they're claws. He bounces toward me, making me jump and squeak like a, well, like a mouse.

He's not lunging or anything, not moving fast, clearly giving me time to adjust, which is good because I freeze in what might be shock and what might be a swelling of hilarity. That lasts for a full two seconds and then I'm running. Running and laughing from a mixture of *what the fuck am I doing* and *this is insanity* and also a realization of just how ridiculous this entire situation is.

It's like I'm ten all over again, playing tag with Chad and Taylor—except we never dressed up like this unless it was Halloween. And I barely know Bryce. So yeah, exactly like that.

The laughter and the headpiece make it hard to see in the dark, and the game has been going on for less than a minute before I trip over something, which may be my own feet. I land on the grass but the extra padding makes the crash tolerable.

And now I'm really laughing my tail off. Bryce is immediately at my side, pulling off his cat head, his eyes full of concern. He's got dark hair cut close. I can't see much else in the dark except the line of his jaw.

"Are you okay?"

"I'm good." I pull off my mouse head and take a few breaths of cool night air. "I can't believe we just did that." I'm still breathless and laughing.

"It was fun, though, right?"

"I . . . It was. I have to be honest, I thought it was strange at first."

He doesn't seem offended at my admission. "Sometimes we forget about having fun purely for the sake of enjoyment. We get scared to be silly, because it's not what's expected. Like just because you're older, you can't do certain things or behave certain ways even though you want to. But who's to say what's fun except you?"

"I guess you're right. I never thought about it. I . . . don't know what I enjoy anymore."

I can't believe those words just popped out of my mouth. Is it true? I don't even know where it came from. It must be true. I don't enjoy journalism but I don't have the courage to go after what I really want.

It's all too scary.

But Bryce doesn't say anything weird or act like I'm nuts, he just nods in understanding.

We sit in silence for a moment. The night air is sharp with the bite of winter but it feels good because the suit is pretty warm.

"I have a whole bunch of furry costumes," he says. "I collect them. I have a whole storage unit for it because I have to hide it from my dad, but we usually go and check them out once a month. All of us. And try different ones on. It's a lot of fun, if you ever wanna come with us and try it out."

"Sure. That would be great."

And then he says, "I'll give you my number." And he pulls out his phone from some compartment in his suit.

Holy shit. It can't be this easy.

"I left my cell inside," I say. "Let me see yours and I'll key my number in. I have removable hands." I pull the detachable gloves off and wiggle my fingers at him.

Goddamn Jude and his brilliant ability to predict things. How does he do it? "That's a great invention."

"It really is."

He hands it over. My heart is pounding. I'm really doing this.

The phone is open to the keypad to enter my number, but I exit out and hit the web browser, keying in the simple address Jude had me memorize. I take a deep breath, waiting for it to load. It probably only takes five seconds but it feels like an eternity.

He can't see what I'm doing from this vantage, but will he notice the bright screen reflected on my furry face? Will this take so long he'll be able to tell?

And then he asks, "So what's up with you and Jude?"

The page loads. I click the download button and watch the spyware install. "Um. Nothing really. We're friends."

Halfway loaded.

His eyes brighten. "So, he's single?"

Fully loaded. The browser closes itself, and I know it's erasing its path, just like Jude said it would.

And it's done. I pass him the phone back, suppressing a grumble. At least the plan worked, but why does everyone and their brother want a chance with Jude? And why am I irritated about it? If they want him, they can have him.

"Yeah. He's single. He has a cat, too, you know. Loves them."

Bryce's grin in the dark is brilliant.

Chapter Nine

There is nothing I would not do for those who are really my friends. I have no notion of loving people by halves, it is not my nature.

—Jane Austen, *Northanger Abbey*

Jude

"I DID IT!" Annabel squeals as soon as we hit the parking lot.

She's so incredibly excited, I hate to stifle her delight, but I place a hand over her arm and put a finger to my lips.

She immediately glances around. "Do you think someone is listening?"

"You can never be too careful. Come on."

We walk in silence to her car and I open the passenger door for her to get in. She had a few drinks after going outside with Bryce and asked me to drive. She's practically vibrating in the seat next to me.

"You did it," I say.

"I totally did! Oh my gosh, it was so nerve racking." She releases a bright laugh.

"I never had any doubts. I knew you could win him over with your sparkling personality."

She snorts. "You're so full of shit. Did you somehow plan all of that?"

"If you mean did I put us into his path, then yes, but you did the rest of the work. Sometimes it is as easy as having a goal and taking steps to ensure success. But if you hadn't agreed to go outside with Bryce, it wouldn't have happened. If he hadn't felt comfortable with you, it wouldn't have happened. How did it play out?"

She explains how Bryce wanted to play cat and mouse and it was so bizarre, but she laughs so freely, more animatedly than I've ever seen her.

She pulls the laughter right outta me, too.

Lightness fills my chest. She doesn't laugh enough. It changes her entire being.

"So, you didn't mind the whole furry thing?"

"It was weird at first, you know. Clearly. But everyone was so nice. It wasn't like I thought it would be. Rachel explained a lot of things to me."

I nod. "They seem like good people. I might go back, actually, for fun. You could come with me. Maybe write something on it for real, you know."

Her brows lift. "I don't know how you do these things."

"Do what things?"

She turns toward me in her seat. "You're so comfortable in any situation. You have so much confidence it's leaking from your pores and infusing the air around you. Everyone wanted to be near you. Rachel. Bryce."

"Really?" I grin. "Does that extend to you?"

She snorts at me and ignores my question. "They all wanted to know if we were together."

"What did you tell them?"

She brushes her hands up and down her jeans. "Not, you know, much."

"You didn't tell Rachel that you and I were an item? Because she seemed to think so."

"Hmm. That's odd." She won't meet my eyes.

"So you weren't threatened by her interest?"

She scoffs. "Of course not."

I choose to let it slide, for now. "You could have confidence leaking from your pores, too. It's not a condition exclusive to me."

"Right, well, it isn't that easy."

"Maybe it is. Make the decision to have a good time, and you will. Understand that you are a fun person to be around, and others will, too."

"But what if people think I'm crazy?"

I lean an elbow on the console between us, moving closer. "Those are their thoughts, not yours. You are the master of your life. You have control over yourself and your reactions to the chaos around you, even if the chaos itself is beyond your reach."

Her eyes are hooded and her gaze flicks down to my mouth.

The action forces my own eyes to her lips, pink and lush, the bottom one slightly fuller than the top.

Slowly, I move my gaze back up to her eyes so there's no confusion about what I want.

For a second, I think she might give in. She even sways toward me.

"Do you want to go back to your place?" she asks.

"Do you want to go to dinner sometime?"

The shutters fall over her eyes and she pulls back. "This again? Come on, Jude. You have to recognize there's a certain tension here." Her hand moves back and forth between us. "And if you want to, you know, relieve the tension, I'm okay with that. But that's all it is. Nothing more."

I sit back in the seat and start the car. "I'll take you on home then." I pull out of the parking lot and she makes it two blocks before she starts talking again.

"You know I don't believe in all that romantic bullshit. Sometimes there's just an itch you need to scratch and nothing more. You know? And together, we would be great . . . scratchers."

"I'll wait until you aren't scared."

"Scared?" She scoffs. "I'm not scared."

"You are. Terrified."

"Of what?"

"Of being emotionally exposed."

She sucks in a breath.

I glance over at her in the passenger seat. As soon as our eyes meet, she crosses her arms over her chest and turns her gaze out the window.

I've pushed too far, but it's too late to take it back.

The rest of the drive is silent. We don't speak further until I've parked in front of her apartment building.

She opens the door to leave, ready to run off without another word.

"I'll call you if I hear anything," I tell her. "And I'll have your car back here by tomorrow morning."

She turns, her eyes searching and wary. She nods once.

I wait until the light clicks on through the window before I drive away.

SUNDAY AFTERNOON, right on cue, there's a honk out in front of the house.

"Granny's here," I call out, but Beast is already walking out the front door.

"Get in, losers, we're making moonshine," she hollers from her 1956 Cadillac convertible. It's a DeVille, and it's pink with gleaming chrome fixtures. Just like the one Elvis used to own.

Granny has sort of adopted us over the last month—in exchange for Beast's brawny assistance. He's a natural at making moonshine, as he is with most culinary-related activities.

And me, well, I'm pretty sure I'm being used for the eye candy and flattery.

Once Beast and I have exited the premises, I lock the front door and walk down the path to her car. "Well I do declare, Mrs. Jackson, you are a sight for sore eyes. Is that a new hat?"

It matches her car. Large and light pink, with a floppy brim and a white flower poking out of one side. The top is off the Cadillac even though it's only about sixty-five degrees.

The hat does not, however, match the rest of her. She's wearing red overalls and a yellow shirt. Giant sunglasses complete her mismatched outfit.

"Don't you try and butter me up, boy. I'm not adding you to my will even if you are handsome as the devil and talk prettier than a preacher at a tent revival. Besides, I'll be outliving you anyway."

I can't help but laugh as I open the passenger-side door while Beast settles his large frame into the back.

The drive is a quiet one on my part because every time I try to make polite conversation, Granny shushes me so she can concentrate on driving, which means she wants to concentrate on waving and yelling at people she knows that we pass on the slow drive through town—which is everyone. And it's slower than normal since she's doing fifteen in a thirty.

"Hey, Prudence, don't forget to cover your roses before it gets too cold! It's likely to get below freezing before next month!"

"Hello, Mr. Thompson! If you're gonna go without a hat, remember to put sunscreen on that shiny head of yours!"

"Elaine! You gonna send me that fried chicken recipe?"

Once there are no more townies to yell at, she speeds up and then hauls tail down the long gravel drive, blowing dust in our wake.

Granny lives in a ranch-style home owned by Reese's parents, Granny's son and his wife.

It's large and comfortable and colorful. The giant ranch house has orange shutters, red trim, blue shingles—and a blindingly yellow rocking chair with a shotgun leaning against it on the porch. The house itself is a reflection of its owners' artistic natures, although they're rarely ever here.

It's like nothing I've ever seen in my life. My parents would have been praying for the Lord's forgiveness for the bright, flamboyant colors. Despite the large and eccentric exterior, it's a welcoming place. In my deepest dreams, I would live somewhere exactly like this with a sassy wife, two point five kids, Mr. Bojangles, and maybe a pig. The most important part would be raising kids who could be themselves. A place where we could share triumphs and failures alike, without fear of judgment or shame. In other words, the exact opposite of my own childhood.

We've barely exited the vehicle when Granny directs me to wait for her in the kitchen and hauls Beast around the house to the barn in back, already yammering about lifting barrels of moonshine and mash.

The door is unlocked, so I let myself inside. The walls are covered with a variety of paintings and murals in vibrant colors, every available surface featuring statues and odd little artifacts and trinkets. A Yoruba goddess poses next to a Zulu warrior king, idols that would make my family cross themselves and hose the whole house down in holy water.

It doesn't take long for Granny to meet me in the kitchen, where she smacks a duster into my hands.

"I need help cleaning the fans and changing some light bulbs that I can't reach. I tried to use the stool but nearly broke my hip. If I'm gonna break my hip, I'd rather it be from doing something fun." She winks.

I chuckle and follow her into the living room, where she points up at the fans. "There's one in the spare room down by the bathroom you can get when you're done with that."

I bow. "I am at your service, my lady."

She smiles and pats my arm. "You keep the cheap flattery coming, too."

After a few, I get the ceiling fans dusted and then once that's done, I find her in the kitchen extracting a pitcher of sweet tea from the fridge.

She's left the bulbs for the lights on the counter and she points out which ones need to be replaced.

Even I have to use a step stool in the high-ceilinged kitchen, and while I'm spinning them in, she asks, "Are you thirsty? I made some sweet tea."

"I would be delighted to partake of your hospitality." I finish with a bulb and step off the stool, turning to face her only to find her already shuffling in my direction. Except she's closer than I realized and we run right into each other and she spills the cold, dark beverage all over my white T-shirt.

"Oh, no. Will you look at that?" She tsks. "What a mess. You're gonna get all sticky. Quick, get that shirt off and I'll put it in the wash. Don't worry, I'll have it clean in a hot minute." She sets the now empty glass down on a nearby counter and holds out her hands for my shirt.

I hesitate, watching her bright eyes. Did she plan this?

Not that I'm complaining. If she wants a show, it's the least I can do. I pull my shirt over my head and puff up my chest a bit, handing over the damp cotton and flexing my arms.

She's grinning like a mule eating briars, and the shirt she was so eager to get in the wash is in her hands but she's not making a move toward the laundry room.

Her eyes are focused below my neck.

Getting ogled by Granny . . . I may have reached a new low.

"Aren't you gonna wash that, ma'am?"

"Sure, sure . . . you need a towel or something?"

"I'm good."

"Yes, yes, you are," she says. "I would offer you a change of shirt but I'm not sure we have any in your size." She grins at me and I can't help but laugh.

"You are slicker than a hound's tooth, Granny."

"Honey, I've been around since dirt was new. Besides, the others should be here soon and I hear Annabel is finally joining us." She reaches into a nearby closet and hands me a broom. "I think the front porch needs some sweeping before they get here, which should be in, oh, 'round about ten minutes."

I shake my head but take the broom from her. I see what she's doing here and I can't say I disapprove.

Chapter Ten

I do not think I ever opened a book in my life which had not something to say upon woman's inconstancy. Songs and proverbs, all talk of woman's fickleness. But perhaps you will say, these were all written by men.

—Jane Austen, *Persuasion*

Annabel

"I'M SO glad you decided to come with us this week. Granny has been asking after you," Reese says as we head down the long gravel drive to the ranch.

I haven't gone to supper at Granny's in a while, always coming up with an excuse because I knew Jude would be there. Granny loves Jude. Everyone loves the rat bastard.

But since I haven't seen him since our last awkward encounter, I wanted to check in without seeming overly desperate by calling (again) or stopping by with some excuse to see Reese for the tenth time.

We've talked on the phone, briefly, but he had nothing new to share.

This whole nefarious spy thing is a lot more boring than I thought it would be. Too much waiting around for Jude to call me and not enough ninja scissor kicking.

Life has been nearly normal. Reese and Fitz are annoyingly sappy, Stan is a jerk, and Bruce keeps telling me things he thinks are inspirational but make no sense, like "A cat can have kittens in the oven, but that don't make 'em biscuits," and "When you find yourself in a hole, stop digging." But at least I haven't had any more threats to my job.

"Did you call Momma yet? She's been asking after you," Fitz says when we stop in front of the house.

Reese is sitting in the middle so I lean over her.

"Don't worry about it, Fitzwilliam. I'll call her."

"Are you sure? Because you keep saying that and you still haven't. She said Dad talked to Bruce the other day and she wants to talk to you about it."

Goddamn small towns. Bruce and Daddy went to high school together. Of course he thinks it's no problem to call my father and talk to him about me and my job. It's not like I'm a legal adult or anything. No ethical conflicts there at all.

Not to mention that all it's gonna do is stress Momma out. I'm stressing enough for the both of us as it is. If I can't pay the rent, there's nowhere else to go. The housing market in Blue Falls is a hot mess ever since the new mines opened outside town. We were lucky to get this place as it is, and there's no money to be had from any other quarter, not since Daddy had to stop working and they moved away to live with our grandma in Florida. Worst-case scenario, we move to Florida with them, which means Fitz wouldn't be able to finish his degree, which is not an option at all.

"It's none of your never mind." I jump out of the truck before he can harass me anymore but then come to a full stop.

Jude is on the porch, sweeping. Shirtless.

Is he trying to kill me?

His chest is defined and built without being overly so. Not too big, not too small, just like a sexy version of Goldilocks.

I follow Reese and Fitz up the walk.

"Granny's got y'all working up a storm, doesn't she?" Reese calls out as we approach.

"She likes to keep me busy." His jeans are slung low on his hips. He leans on the broom, all relaxed grace and intrinsic masculinity wrapped in a muscular package.

And somehow he's a light golden color everywhere. Where and when has he been tanning? Does he go to a salon? He's a hacker. They aren't supposed to be golden gods with six-packs. They're supposed to be milky white with saggy moobs and spindly arms.

"Where's your shirt?" I ask.

"Granny had a little accident with the sweet tea."

Fitz laughs. "I just bet she did."

Granny opens the door. "There's my little Tootsie Roll. Heya, Fitz, Annabel. I'm fixin' to set the table, since the food's 'bout done. Reese, why don't you help me?"

"Sure, Granny."

She heads inside and then Granny focuses on Fitz.

"Would you mind checking on Beast? He's in the barn, straining the mash."

"On it." Fitz disappears around the side of the house.

And just like that, I'm left alone on the porch with a shirtless, broom-wielding, too-sexy-for-his-own-good Jude Parker.

I'm trying not to stare, but it's damn near impossible.

One of his pecs tightens and flexes under my scrutiny.

"Stop that!"

"Then stop staring." He's grinning.

"Aren't you cold?" I pick at nonexistent fuzz on my sleeve.

He shrugs. "It's like sixty-five degrees. Not exactly sweater weather."

"In East Texas, anything lower than seventy-two is sweater weather."

We fall silent. His eyes are bright as the sky with the sun behind me, and the weight of his gaze makes me squirm. He's watching me and I'm trying to watch anything but him. He's doing that thing where he says nothing to try and make me uncomfortable and cave first, and dammit, it's working.

"Have you heard anything?"

"Nothing worth mentioning. I would have called you."

"Uh-huh."

"Don't you trust me?" He moves closer.

Now him and his hot man chest are within touching distance. My stomach shimmers in anticipation. I want to touch him. I want him to touch me. I'm like one of those toys in the package with the button, touch to test. "Should I?"

"I don't see why not."

He's so close, all that skin and muscle makes my mouth goes dry. He has a smattering of freckles on his shoulders. Why is he so hot?

My hand rises of its own volition, as if he's answering my internal question. *Yes, touch to test, go ahead.* I yank my disobedient fingers back, covering my mouth on a cough, as if that's what I had intended all along.

"You need some water, darlin'?"

"I need something."

His grin is slow and sends heat rippling through me.

"Jude! Annabel! Dinner!" Granny calls.

I jump back a mile, but Jude just smiles at me, lazily, while I fluster and fiddle with my clothes like a teen getting caught necking by her parents.

Jude motions for me to precede him into the house. He follows, close as a shadow.

Beast and Fitz are sitting at the table while Reese and Granny bring out some dishes from the kitchen.

We all sit around the long table in the substantial dining room, but while sizeable, it's not formal. The chandelier over the table is a mishmash of geometrical shapes and primary colors. The seats are bench style, formed with a dark gleaming wood that matches the table. I slide in next to Beast, and Jude sits on my other side. Very closely on my other side.

Granny sits at the head of the table and says grace before we dig in. When she passes a dish down to Jude and it nearly spills on him, he asks, "Is my shirt ready yet?"

She purses her lips in thought, her head cocking to one side like she's listening for the wash. "I don't think so."

Amusement lightens his tone. "How long does it take to wash and dry one shirt?"

She busies herself with the silverware and napkin in front of her. "It's possible and somewhat likely I may have forgotten to move it to the dryer."

"I have an extra shirt in my truck," Fitz offers.

Granny gives him the stink eye, but Fitz ignores it and runs out to the truck and comes back with a Blue Falls track shirt. Jude tugs it over his head and covers all that perfect virility. I can't help but sigh in relief.

Now I can focus on something else. Except Fitz is a runner and longer and leaner than Jude, so the shirt is a bit too small and tight around his chest and now Jude is sitting a smidge closer.

Our thighs are touching.

I'm not moving away first, dammit.

Granny asks everyone—except Jude and me—about school.

I listen and shovel mashed potatoes and pulled pork into my mouth while Fitz and Reese assure Granny they're getting ready for finals and staying on top of their obligations, and Jude comments on Beast's excellent grades and test-taking abilities.

Then she lasers in on Reese, as she does, about how much time she's spending with Fitz and how their relationship is progressing.

Normally, I'd join in and argue with Granny or tease Reese because it's fun, but I'm too focused on the man next to me. I can't stop thinking about the heat of his leg pressed against mine, or the way he wipes his mouth with the napkin, or the feel of his arm brushing mine.

Granny says, "You can't ignore the physical aspects of a relationship."

My belly dips in response to Jude's low chuckle.

Wait. That pulls me back. "What are we talking about?"

But now I've yanked the spotlight from Reese, who throws me a grateful smile, not realizing the move was completely unintentional.

"Annabel. How's work? Any good gossip I should know about?" Granny asks.

Something buzzes in Jude's pocket, the vibration moving through my thigh since he's basically on top of me. Surreptitiously, so only his hand is moving and anyone on the other side of the table can't even tell, he pulls the small phone out of his pocket and lays it face up in his lap.

"It's great. Nothing really going on. The usual stuff, you know."

"Nothing to share? Can't swing a cat in this town without hitting someone with juicy gossip and you should have the best being at the *Daily*."

"Uh." I glance over at Jude. The happy-go-lucky smile is gone. His eyes are serious.

Something is happening.

We need to get out of here.

"Actually, speaking of the paper, I just remembered I

have to go to . . . um, do something for that right now." I stand up and glance over at Fitz. "Can I take your truck?"

He's bewildered. Understandably. "You have to leave now? We haven't even had dessert yet."

"I don't mean to be rude, but it's for my job. And you know, it's important because we have to pay bills and such."

"Where do you have to go?" Reese asks.

Jude stands. "Actually, it's for me."

Fitz leans back, crossing his arms over his chest and scrutinizing both of us. "For you? Really, guys? Ads for gigolos doing well these days?" His words are joking, but his tone is hard around the edges.

"I've got a little interest with the paper and Annabel is assisting me," Jude says. "But we can't talk about it yet, because, you know, ethics and sources and all that."

Reese cocks her head at us, a little smile on her face, but Fitz is still blinking in confusion.

"That makes literally no sense."

"It's one of my many lucrative ventures, babies. You know how I am with my entrepreneurial mindset. Now if you'll excuse us, we have some business to attend to."

"Y'all can take my car," Granny says. "Keys are by the door. Bring it back by tomorrow afternoon. I have an appointment at the beautician. And I expect you to make up for this absence by coming over for supper on Thanksgiving. No excuses."

"Yes, ma'am," Jude says.

"Clothing optional," Granny adds.

Jude smiles at her and kisses her on her white-haired head.

"Thanks, Granny," I say, giving her a hug and then following Jude out the door.

I'm buckling up in the front seat of Granny's Cadillac when I ask, "What did you find out?"

"Bryce received a phone call from a blocked number. Might be something important."

He drives us through town, his hands competent and strong on the steering wheel. Within ten minutes, we're back at his place. "You need water or anything?" he asks as we pass the kitchen.

"Uh, no, thanks."

He's always so damn considerate. It makes him even sexier.

Once in his room, he shuts the door behind us and heads to his closet, pulling out his laptop and flipping it open on his desk, fingers flying.

With a few clicks, he starts the playback.

"Hey. You wanted me to call?" Bryce's voice, but the pitch is high and wavery.

"You alone?" the other voice asks. It's male and young and confident. Louder than Bryce. No nerves here. Definitely a Texas drawl, too.

"Yeah."

"I need you to make a delivery."

"Where?"

"Pick up will be in the same place as last time. Get it by eight tomorrow night and bring it to Bodean's. They've got a computer in the office 'round back. Just stick it in the drive and it will run its magic."

"Fine. But this is the last time I'm doing this." Bryce

tries to sound tough, but his voice is on the shrill side of nervous.

The voice on the other line chuckles, and what should be a humorous sound has a dark edge. “It’s the last time when I say it is. I’ve got you by the balls, little boy. If you don’t help me, not only will I reverse your grades, I bet daddy dearest would love to know everything you’ve been up to lately.” There’s a smile wrapped around the bitter words and the hairs on the back of my neck rise.

“But, but, I—”

Click.

Bryce emits a gargled sound of frustration and hangs up.

Jude and I share a glance.

“Bodean’s.”

I shake my head. “The Turkey Trot is tomorrow night. It’s a charity dance competition. They hold it there every year. It’s very popular and the place will be packed.”

Jude’s eyes light up.

“Now you want to have a dance competition some night, don’t you?

“Well now, that would be a fine way to generate some income.” Jude taps away at his laptop.

“Whoever Bryce was talking to sounded young. Like early twenties, maybe.” I sit on the edge of the desk, watching him work. Competent fingers flying.

Jude nods, his brow furrowed. “Sounded vaguely familiar. You think?”

“I didn’t recognize it.”

“We’ll have to go to Bodean’s tomorrow and see what our little furry friend has gotten into.”

I frown. "He's not a bad guy."

"I would like to believe so, but we can't know that."

"He seemed so nervous. The other voice, though, sounded confident. And what he said, about reversing Bryce's grades? Spilling stuff to his dad? It sounds to me like he's being blackmailed."

"Even people being blackmailed have a choice. Whatever he's doing, he doesn't have to. He's complicit."

"But he has stuff to lose, maybe. Don't you think?"

"Does that matter when you're choosing between right and wrong?"

"Oh, come on, you're the one that's all 'it's okay for Grace to break the law if it's for the benefit of her and Beast,' right?"

"I know." He grins. "I just like to argue with you. Riling you up and seeing you all mad has become a favorite pastime of mine. And I know you enjoy it, too."

Damn him. I do. "Ugh." I smack him lightly.

"Ouch." He rubs his shoulder.

"Oh, please."

"You've wounded me."

"I will wound you."

Our eyes meet and lock and the ever-present tension flames to life between us.

I take a breath and step away. "What's the plan?"

"We know where he's gonna be tomorrow night, in the office of Bodean's. So we'll just get there before he does."

"And then what?"

He shrugs. "I usually improvise these things."

"Improvise? Not this again! We need a plan."

"You can't control everything, least of all other people.

I want to know what's on this drive and who is blackmailing our friend Bryce. Those are our two main objectives. Whoever this guy is, he's using other people and other IPs to cover his tracks."

"Do you think Grace will be there?"

"I don't know. I suppose we'll find out."

Chapter Eleven

But we loved with a love that was more than love—
I and my Annabel Lee
—Edgar Allen Poe, "Annabel Lee"

Jude

"WHAT ARE YOUR INTENTIONS WITH ANNABEL?"

I move my gaze from the TV, where I've been watching *Love Actually*, and turn to Fitz.

He's next to me on the couch, leaning back, one arm over the end of the couch, and his posture relaxed except for the tension in his shoulders.

"I can assure you, my intentions are always honorable."

"Uh-huh. Look, I know you guys are going out tonight. Annabel told me she's picking you up and I'm not invited."

"It's just a friendly night out."

"Great. Then why can't I come?"

"I'm afraid it's more about business than pleasure and you wouldn't have a good time."

Fitz rolls his eyes. "I get it. You like her, but I think Annabel likes you, too."

I lift my brows. "And this is a problem?"

He shifts in his seat, leaning forward and running his palms over his jeans before meeting my eyes. "I've been getting the sense that there's something else going on there. I think you like her and even more scarily, I think she likes you back."

I shrug. "I don't profess to know what the fair Annabel feels or doesn't feel."

"I know Annabel better than anyone and she puts on a good show, but she's actually very sensitive and hurts easily."

"I understand what you're saying."

"Understand this as well: if you hurt my sister, I'll hurt you."

I smile. They're both so protective of each other. It's endearing. Admirable. "I think it's more likely she'll hurt me."

He nods. "That could be true. She can be meaner than a wet panther."

There's a knock at the front door and then it's opened. "Hello?" Annabel calls out.

I stand up but before I make it out of the living room, she's already in the doorway and I think my heart straight stops, and in the resulting silence I can do naught but stare.

She's not showing a lot of skin, dressed in a pale green country dress. The hem falls above the knee, flirting with her thighs, and brown cowboy boots cover her feet. But she's a cool drink of water on a hot summer day and I want more than anything to drink her up.

"Hey." She smiles at me.

The rare glimpse of happiness gives me encouragement.

"You look mighty fine tonight, Annabel. You could talk the dogs off a meat truck without having to say a word."

She blushes. She never blushes. I want to chase the pink spreading down her chest and see where it ends. Her walls are always too high to show such a display of pleasure. And the fact that they've been knocked down, even for a moment, is a win.

"You're not so bad yourself."

I glance down at my plain red flannel, jeans, and boots. It's not much, but she approves. The problem is getting her to approve of the man inside the body.

"Although . . ." Annabel purses her lips, walking over to me and reaching out. My breath catches in my throat. She unbuttons the top snap on my shirt. "You're a little too put together for Bodean's." She runs a hand through my scruffy hair. Her fingers feel divine and I nearly groan out loud. She's so close I can see individual eyelashes, and one glance in a general downward direction gives me an eyeful of cleavage.

Eyes up, buck.

Fitz clears his throat and she turns away, apparently done with my impromptu makeover, which is good because I have some adjusting to do below the buckle. One little voluntary touch from Annabel, and I'm a goner in more ways than one.

"Hey, Mr. Darcy." Annabel hugs Fitz.

"Hey, sis. You kids have fun and be safe tonight, ya hear?"

Annabel rolls her eyes. "As your elder, I think that's my line."

"You're only three years older than me."

"Whatever, puppy. You ready?" she asks me.

I nod. I just have to grab my laptop and put it in her trunk and then we're on our way.

Bodean's is an old barn that's been fitted with a porch and refurbished into a bar. People spill out of the front, the twang of a guitar and the beat of country music filling the night air as we walk up the wooden steps and inside.

It's as packed as it sounded from outside. Annabel stays on the perimeter of the crowd while I battle the line at the bar to obtain some refreshments. We don't want to stick out like sore thumbs, have to make it seem at least somewhat like we belong here.

When I finally have drinks in hand and I'm heading back to where I left Annabel, she's not alone anymore.

I don't recognize the gentleman at first because he's not in his normal Blue Falls police uniform, but as I approach, the moustache and wide smile become more familiar. Officer Rudy.

"Come on now, Annabel, just one little dance."

"Thanks, but no thanks."

An unfamiliar sensation rolls over me. I don't like him asking her to dance. I know she can take care of herself, but I can't help the possessiveness from reaching out and curling an arm around Annabel's waist.

When her eyes meet mine, her shoulders relax and she leans closer, as close as she's ever willfully gotten, and that's all the assent I need to hand her the drink I procured.

"Officer Rudy. It's a pleasure to see you again." I've only met the man twice, but I've gotten the impression he is someone who craves attention and never receives enough to fill the bucket.

He glances back and forth between the two of us.

"Nice to see you, as well," he mumbles and then makes excuses of some sort and smiles tightly before disappearing into the crowd.

"He bother you a lot?"

She shrugs. "Not a bother. It's Rudy. He's like that to everyone."

I frown and take a small sip of beer while assessing the rest of the room.

People participating in the Turkey Trot are identifiable by their turkey gear, some with T-shirts of turkeys, some with feathered hats and wings. Rudy is now across the way, conversing with another lady who smiles and moves away. Apparently he's getting rejected all around. No sign of Grace or Bryce, or anyone else who appears suspicious.

The music kicks up, "Turkey in the Straw" from the sound of it, and a chorus of cheers fills the space.

The dance floor fills. Now is the time. I nudge Annabel with an elbow and we move along the far wall, where it's not as crowded, toward the restrooms at the back.

The hallway is darkened, only a bit of illumination coming from the bar and dance area. It's thankfully empty since nearly everyone is on the dance floor.

A patron disappears into the bathroom in front of us and we wait until the door swings shut before trying the door opposite.

Locked.

"Wait, I got this." Annabel plucks a pin from her hair and bends over the knob.

"I suppose this is how you got into my bedroom before I purchased additional locks?"

"What? Like it's hard?" The tumblers fall and she pushes the door open. After a quick glance, we go inside, shutting and locking the door behind us as she flicks on the light.

There's a ladylike scream.

And standing there, hands on the keyboard, is Bryce.

"What are you guys doing here?" Bryce's sentence ends on a squeak.

"Babies!" I throw on my alter ego. "We came here to party!" I grin at him like he's expected and not performing some kind of reprehensible activity. "Are you . . . what are you doing?" The frown on my face morphs into a perfect reflection of confused perplexity.

"Nothing. Just, um. Working. I work here."

I step closer. "In the dark?"

"I . . . I get migraines."

Annabel jumps into the conversation. "There's no need to lie, Bryce. We already know. He told us. We were surprised because we thought you would be here a little later since he said to pick up the item by eight and it's not even eight thirty. He asked us to check on you and help if needed."

Annabel is pretending like she already knows everything. Clever. I would kiss her if I thought she would allow it and the circumstances were different.

"Help me with what?"

"Uploading the file." I move over to the computer where Bryce is standing and watch the screen as the program uploads. I am unable to tell what it is at first glance. The computer itself is an older model Dell. It doesn't even have thumb drive capabilities, which means there's a disc in the drive. And whatever it is, it's taking forever to upload.

Bryce rubs a hand through his dark hair. "But it's only a few buttons and once it's done, I can leave. Why would he need you to be here?"

We share a glance and then Annabel bites her lip and gives Bryce a pitying grimace. "He wanted us to come get the goods when it was done. To bring it back to him."

"Oh."

"Yeah. He said something about how you didn't want to help him anymore, or something? He wasn't real happy."

Bryce's eyes flick to me and Annabel. "Do you know what's on this thing?"

"You don't?" I ask.

He frowns. "David only gives me minimal information."

Pause. David, huh? That's useful.

"Why do you do these things for him?" Annabel asks.

He glances down, runs a hand through his hair in frustration. "I . . . can't really say. Why are you helping him?"

"We don't really have a choice anymore." She sighs. Totally playing on his sympathy. The urge to kiss her returns with a vengeance. "What is he holding over you?"

Bryce's whole body droops. "It's not my fault Professor Stewart is a jerk. He failed me because I had a group project and my whole team bailed. David told me he would get me a C. He changed my grade somehow." He gestures to the computer. "He's really good at the hacker stuff. But then I owed him a favor in exchange. I did the favor. It was just a pickup and delivery. Simple. I thought that was it and I would be done, but then it turned into one thing after another. I tried to stop, but he told me he could reverse my grades any time he wanted and then he found out about the furry stuff, and that gave him one more thing to hold over me. I didn't know it would get this far but . . . you have to understand, I can't fail out of college."

"What else has he made you do in exchange for his help?"

The disc finally finishes uploading and before Bryce can do anything, I hit the eject button and slip it in my front pocket.

Bryce watches but doesn't make any moves to stop me. "Usually not much. He has me run errands around town, uploading things like this to different computers. Sometimes public ones, like at the library. I don't want to do it anymore, though. Some of this stuff could be bad and I wouldn't even know. It doesn't feel right. Can you talk to him? Tell him to leave me alone? I thought he was a normal guy, but he's . . . off. It's like he enjoys having this sick power over me."

There's a jiggle at the door and we all freeze. Bryce slides like a smooth slip of jelly down under the desk.

I move toward Annabel, who's standing near the door, staring down at it like it might bite.

"There's nowhere to hide," she hisses, eyes wide.

Whoever is at the door has a key. The handle turns. She flicks off the light and I press her back against the wall, my arms on either side of her head, moving my face as close as I can without actually making contact, tilting my head toward her neck so close her heat presses against me. To anyone behind us it would appear rather indecent, but in reality, I'm not even touching her.

I breathe in the scent of cherry mixed with a faint whiff of perfume.

Her own breathing is affected, sharp and shallow.

Light floods the room and a voice asks, "What in Sam Hill are y'all doing in here?"

I pull away, turning from Annabel's flushed face to ask. "What? Who are you?"

Annabel steps out from the cage of my arms and glances around in confusion. "This isn't the bathroom?" she asks in a breathy voice and then turns back to me and grabs my shirt. "You are so hot." She presses herself against me.

"This was supposed to be locked," the man at the door drawls. I recognize him from the bar. Tall cowboy. He yells down the hall toward the bar, "Eliza, did you forget to lock the office again?"

"Fuck you, Ranger, I locked it!" a voice yells back.

"Yeah right," he mutters. "She always says that."

I nudge Annabel. "We'll be getting out of your hair then."

She hangs on to me like she can barely stand, stumbling over her boots. We make it past the cowboy and out the door without further incident. Once we're out of sight, she straightens and pulls away. "Should we help Bryce?"

"I think he'll survive. We can help him most by getting our hands on David."

Her eyes meet mine. "You know who it is?"

"I think I do. He attends my parties. I thought I recognized the voice." I glance around. We need to get somewhere else and see what's on this disc. "Let's get out of here."

The bar is loud and the thump of feet on the dance floor echoes around us. She leads the way through a row of empty, narrowly spaced tables.

Then she stops suddenly in front of me.

I wait a few beats, but she doesn't move.

"Annabel?"

No response.

"Are you okay?" I move to put a hand on her shoulder, but before I can make contact, she drops to the ground.

Chapter Twelve

"Are people so unhappy when they love?"

"Yes, Christine, when they love and are not sure of being loved."

—Gaston Leroux, *The Phantom of the Opera*

Annabel

YOU KNOW, the floor seemed like the best option at the time, but now that I'm staring down at a wooden compilation of crumbs, dirt, sticky beer, and other questionable liquids, I'm not sure if standing and making eye contact with Taylor and Chad was actually worse.

It was a slice of hell seeing Taylor the other day at work and finding out she and Chad are getting married.

But seeing them now? Gazing at each other like the end of some sappy romance movie? I'd rather get a root canal.

Chad was behind Taylor, his arms around her waist, leaning down, saying something in her ear. She laughed and looked over her shoulder at him, eyes bright and happy and mouth wide and smiling.

And then her eyes locked with mine.

So uncomfortable.

Although . . . I wonder if this should hurt more.

I mean, it does, and yet not like it did when I thought Chad should be mine. It hurts because they were both mine. My best friends.

And now they're not.

And the reality of it is so sad.

"What are we doing? You okay? You need me to carry you?" Jude is behind me, also crouched down. I nearly forgot he was there. Of course, instead of thinking I'm a total freak, he is all gentlemanly concern.

"No," I say. "I just need a second here."

"Alrighty then, we can sit here on the floor that smells like piss and beer until you're ready. Or maybe we're pretending to be frogs? I can leapfrog you from here or you can go first if you'd like me to turn around."

Insane laughter bubbles up inside and I turn my head to meet his eyes. Somehow, he's completely natural, crouching on the floor, his eyes serious despite his teasing words.

"What is it?" he asks.

"It's . . ." Can I tell him without feeling humiliated? Unlikely. Although he's probably the only person in the world I could share this part of me with who wouldn't judge or scorn or reject me. I still can't believe all he's shared with me, trusted me with. How much he's trusted me not to hurt him.

I could trust him, too.

The thought staggers me into momentary silence.

"Annabel?" a familiar voice says from above, pulling me from my inner revelation. The absolute last voice I want to hear.

Taylor and Chad are both staring down at me with concern in their eyes.

"Can we talk?" Taylor crosses her arms. Then uncrosses them. Then crosses them again. I almost laugh because it's exactly what she did when we were in high school and she was nervous and had to talk in front of the whole class for a presentation in political science. I teased her mercilessly. She's terrible at public speaking. And confrontation. Always has been. And yet, here she is, trying to talk to me despite my past rebuffs.

Before I can respond to her question, Jude saves me.

"Found it!" He stands, pretending to put something in his eye before nodding at Taylor. "I lost my contact and Annabel here was courteous enough to help me attempt to locate it. Hi, I'm Jude Parker. You may have heard of me." He sticks out a hand.

I get to my feet next to him, watching the act he's perfected over the last six months. It's like there's two of him, the real Jude and this public persona he pulls out and shrugs on when he needs it, like a winter coat.

"Hi, I'm Taylor. This is my . . . Chad. This is Chad."

Jude shakes both their hands and they make idle chitchat, Jude oozing charm and politeness, while I stand there in a daze, not really listening.

Is this really happening?

"It's a real pleasure to meet you folks. Are y'all competing out there tonight?"

"Oh, we just came for fun to watch and stuff, you know." Taylor smiles at him. "Support a good cause."

"Well that's mighty kind of you. Now if y'all will excuse us, I put my contact back in after it was swirling in something questionable on the floor and now it's burning like the dickens and we should probably get to the ER. Nice meeting you folks." And then he steps up behind me and I nearly melt into him. "You ready to go, darlin'?" he purrs into the shell of my ear.

If I wasn't such a hot mess, I might say something about the darlin', since the real reason I detest the endearment is because it makes something twist and tighten in my chest.

But he distracted them. He knew I didn't want to talk to them and he made it all go away.

A sudden well of emotion rises inside, but I ram it back down. This time, it doesn't go down easy. It's like the cave in my mind is stuffed with angry elephants, and the bats are ready to start them stampeding.

I nod and make an awkward wave to Taylor and Chad and then we're moving out. Taylor's face is drawn. Chad enfolds her in his arms and her eyes shut but then they blink open and meet mine.

My stomach is in turmoil, the drink I had at the bar curdling among all the tension and emotion I've worked so hard for so long to suppress.

We walk in silence to my little Honda.

Jude puts a gentle hand on my arm and asks, "Do you want me to drive?"

I've been standing there, staring at the driver's side door for probably longer than a minute. I can't formulate a response and in the end I don't have to.

"Don't worry, I'll get you home."

There's nothing I want more. Except pizza, a gallon of ice cream, three hot dogs, and maybe some mind-numbing whiskey.

It's a testament to my mental instability that I hand him the keys without argument or question. Handing over control like it isn't the only thing I've been hanging on to for the past four years.

He opens the passenger door for me and then we're driving in silence through the quiet, dark streets of Blue Falls.

Memories swirl in my mind.

In first grade, I found Taylor, pigtails and overalls, hiding in the library from the mean girls during lunch. I shared my snack pack with her.

She was my first and best friend.

I could tell her anything, like the time we were doing fitness testing in sophomore-year gym class. Brett Adams—one of the hottest guys in school—was holding my feet while I attempted as many sit-ups as I could muster in one minute and I farted on him, basically right in his face. I was so mortified I left school sick, but then Taylor came over that night with pizza and my favorite apple pie from the diner. She could always make a horrible experience seem not so bad.

The regrets are enough to consume my entire being. I

miss her. I miss our friendship. I try to reach for the anger that held the sorrow at bay in the past, that simmering righteous indignation toward both of them that kept me safe from feeling too sad.

They lied. And it's not my fault they ruined everything. All for what? A serotonin trip that doesn't exist except in fantasyland?

I blink and we've made it back to my apartment. Jude walks with me to the door after getting his laptop out of the back.

Once we're inside, he sets his computer on the small coffee table and I sit on the couch. It's quiet and dark. Jude flicks on the light in the kitchen but the living room is still shadowed, only catching a glow from the next room. Fitz must be with Reese. The apartment is quiet and empty. Jude must've known, that's why we came here instead of going to his place. And why he brought his computer. He's always prepared.

Jude emerges with a glass of water and I drink it. After a few long, quiet minutes, I glance over at him.

He's got his glasses on again, the glow from the laptop highlighting his face, the glare hiding his eyes, but I can still see his lips. He rubs his beard absentmindedly and sucks his full lower lip in between his teeth and something in my stomach heats and flips simultaneously.

I remember the feel of those lips, how amazing he was at kissing, how turned on I was before he ruined it with sweet emotion.

Damn his lips. And those glasses. That's what lured me in the last time. He's so geeky and yet so hot and it's impossible to resist. He's . . . geektastic.

His fingers tap away at lightning speed. He's already stuck the disc in and done something with it, and now he pops it out of the drive and puts it on the coffee table in front of us.

I clear my throat. "Anything good on there?"

His head lifts and our eyes connect. Bright and intense and serious. "It's a small part of Grace's program. It has her written all over it, her signature embedded into the code. And I can date it to less than a week ago. Somehow this David guy got ahold of it. I know him. David O'Flannigan."

He turns the laptop so I can see. The picture is from his student ID. He's young, early twenties, medium-brown hair, smarmy smile . . . He looks vaguely familiar, but most people in Blue Falls do.

I lift my eyes to meet Jude's. "How do you know him?"

"He comes to all my events." He taps a few more keys and then smirks. "He's majoring in computer science. And he's stupidly prominent on social media." He rubs his hands together. "This is going to be easy. Too easy."

"What do you mean?"

"All I have to do is schedule something with the babies to lure him over and we can question him."

"Are you gonna torture intel out of him?"

"Won't be necessary. He enjoys blackmailing others, so he understands how it works. I know I can find enough to beat him at his own game. Starting with this." He lifts the disc in the air.

I smile at his enthusiasm. "Nice."

He goes back to tapping away. "Isn't it, though?" he

murmurs, his attention already moving on to whatever he's doing on the computer.

It's quiet except for the hum of the fridge kicking on in the kitchen and the rapid click of his keyboard. In the faint light, his eyes are focused and steady. I want to know what he looks like under the beard. I wonder if he has a firm jaw.

He has good structure in his face, thick lips, a patrician nose, high cheekbones.

After a minute of squirming, I finally muster up my courage. "Jude?"

His eyes lift from the screen.

"Thank you."

He smiles, a small tilt of one side of his mouth. "No thanks necessary." He glances around, as if realizing we're sitting in a mostly dark room alone while he works and I sit here and drool over him. I wipe my mouth to double-check.

Okay, good. Inside. I'm drooling on the inside.

I rub my hands on my dress. He's so calm and put together and collected. Nothing seems to bother him. And, of course, he had to witness my meltdown. How can he be sitting there all blasé when he's in the room alone with a complete psycho?

Because he's not like everyone else. You can tell him the truth, a little voice inside me whispers. It would be so nice to drop the mask and let all the truth out.

"You must think I'm crazy."

"Not at all."

He knows what I'm talking about, doesn't even faze

him. "Are you going to ask why I went bonkers there for a hot second?"

"I would never pry. You choose what you tell me. It's not my right to know. It would be an honor if you trusted me enough to share, but I would never push you." He leans toward me. "And I would never judge you, Annabel. We all have things in our past that make us feel shameful. You are more than the sum of your past experiences. I know that more than most."

I blink at him in the dim light, sincerity radiating from him like warm rays from spring sunshine.

I remember how he was the other night at the furry thing, throwing himself into the situation with abandon, without judgment or condescension. He's not the type to belittle. He didn't scoff at me when I ninja crawled on a dirty bar floor. He helped Reese and Fitz even though they both have their own peccadillos. He takes care of Beast. He's helping Grace not for himself, but because he actually cares. He would be someone so easy to talk to. To . . . feel for.

I don't want to do it. I don't want to get any closer to him than I already am, but I can't stop it. I can't keep the elephants calm any longer. Maybe I can release the story and it will lose its ever-present hold on me. I won't feel like such a fool, such an idiot for making a mistake and an even worse one for holding on to it for so long.

I stand up and hold out my hand.

He stares at it for a long moment before sliding his fingers into mine. He stands, leaving the laptop on the couch, and I lead him down the hall to my bedroom.

The bedside lamp is small, but it gets the job done. I

click it on and head over to my closet. Behind my work clothes and T-shirts, on the floor under my suitcase, there's an old shoebox.

I grab it and turn around.

My room is smaller with Jude in it, as if his very presence fills up the whole space.

He's standing in front of my bulletin board of faraway places, his eyes taking in everything before moving to the pictures of Fitz and my parents on the dresser, and then he turns and our eyes meet.

He sits on the bed.

Standing in front of him, I open the box and hand him a picture. It's Taylor and me before our first seventh-grade dance. I'm wearing a black dress from a thrift store. My hair is a wild mess and I stole some of Momma's dark eyeliner. I look like something out of a gothic novel. Taylor's wearing a bright sundress, no makeup, her hair perfectly curled. We're leaning into each other and laughing.

"Taylor was, she was . . . we were best friends."

I pull out another picture, this one from high school. Standing outside the school, Chad is between us in his dark blue football jersey. "Chad was our friend, too, but Taylor and I were friends first. Since first grade."

Jude takes the photo, his pointer finger stopping next to my smiling face.

"In seventh grade, Chad moved here from Colorado. He saw Taylor and me playing Magic: the Gathering and immediately wanted in on the game."

Jude smiles. "I love that game."

Of course he does. I return his smile before continuing. "You have to understand, Blue Falls is a small town and the schools are tiny. I attended preschool through high school with roughly the same thirty kids. And Chad, he was this blond-haired, blue-eyed, athletic . . . treasure. All the girls thought he was the hottest, newest, shiniest thing. But he wanted to hang with us, the nerds, instead of the more popular girls. We were almost immediately inseparable. All through middle school and high school, we were like the three musketeers, except better." I search my mind for a comparison. "We were Harry, Ron, and Hermione. We loved books and fandoms and each other."

I sit on the edge of the bed because here's where it goes downhill and I need something sturdy for support.

"Things started changing a little, for me, near the end of high school."

I don't know where to focus so I stare down at my cowboy boots, the toes scuffed from use. I bought them five years ago with Taylor. We drove all the way to the Boot Barn in Shreveport to get them.

"I developed this massive crush on Chad. It started the end of junior year of high school. We all went to the homecoming dance together and the last dance it was Chad and me. He held me close and we swayed under the cheap streamers to some sappy love song. It was no big deal, he was like a brother but then he made a comment like we fit so well together with my head just under his chin, and something sort of shifted inside me. I'm sure it was mostly hormones combined with all the confusion that comes from being a teenager. But after that night, I saw him differently. Maybe I was looking for what I wanted to see. But I really thought I loved him. I mean, I did love him. But I thought it was more than the friendship love that we all had for each other."

I search his face but there's no judgment. His face is open and intent and engaged. It gives me the strength to continue.

"And just like that, the entire dynamic of our friendship changed. At least, for me. I told Taylor, eventually, but I kept it to myself until college. I wanted him, but I was sure he didn't feel the same way and I was so young and insecure. Taylor didn't really encourage me, but she listened and she agreed I shouldn't say anything to mess it up.

"But then, one day, Chad kept asking me odd questions about Taylor. Like what was her favorite flower, her favorite place to eat dinner—he totally grilled me. I was sure something was going on with them, but when I confronted Taylor, she got defensive and told me that I'd just misunderstood. That Chad told her he wanted me, not her, and he was just using her as an excuse. And of course, I believed her. I had no reason to not trust her. She'd never been deceitful. Not ever.

"Then one day a few weeks later, just before sophomore year, he said he wanted to talk to me alone and I thought this was it, it was happening. He was going to tell me how much he loved me. I got all dressed up. Put on extra makeup. Oh God." I cover my face with a hand and am doubly embarrassed to find my fingers shaking. I've never told anyone this and now I'm telling Jude, of all people. "This is so embarrassing."

I pull my hand from my face and set it on the bed, and Jude's hand covers mine. I can't possibly meet his eyes, so I stare down at our hands, his long warm fingers strong and gently encouraging. The bedspread underneath us is a dark blue comforter I've had since college. I had it on my bed even then, the day everything changed. "He came over. He was alone. And before he could say anything, I spilled it all. I was so nervous. I went on and on about how much I loved him and wanted to be with him. How I was so happy he was finally in the same place, too."

I grimace and pull away, wrapping both arms around my stomach, like it will somehow stop the queasy memory from taking root. "Chad . . . he sat there and listened, stunned. He let me go on and on, did nothing to stop me from spewing all my emotional diarrhea all over him." I swallow and glance over at Jude. He's listening, his face serious and unreadable, his bright eyes somehow warm.

"And then he said, in the kindest voice possible, that he was in love with Taylor. And she was in love with him. It was almost worse than if he had laughed or something. He was . . . so sympathetic. He felt bad for me. They'd been seeing each other for months. Months, nearly a year, since before I'd told Taylor about my own feelings, and they'd hid it from me. They'd lied to me. And Taylor, that was the worst part, because I had told her everything. She knew how I felt and she lied right to my face. And here I was, spilling out my whole heart and letting it bleed all over the floor and all along, he and Taylor had been sneaking around behind my back." I stop and laugh a little. "That's not entirely right, like Chad and I were a couple and Taylor got between us and it wasn't like that, but they were my best friends. Taylor was my best friend. We had no secrets. Or I thought we didn't. She had been lying to me, so it felt that way. You know?"

He nods but otherwise doesn't interrupt.

"He had asked me those questions because he and Taylor had been hiding, but they were gonna tell me. He wanted to take her out to celebrate because they hadn't gone on a real date even though they'd been hooking up for like, ever. He thought I would be happy. He told me all that, so matter-of-fact, so much like Chad." I laugh, but the sound holds no humor. "Chad is a nice guy. He's like this cliché of someone in a high school movie. All-American football player, blond good looks, a gentle soul, but sometimes he can be so dense."

I have to take a moment to swallow after uttering such a monumental understatement.

"But not this time. This time it was me. I felt so foolish. I was a dumb kid with a crush and they were having this whole serious adult relationship. I walked out of my own apartment that day, just left Chad behind. Taylor and I were roommates even, but I left and never went back. I went all the way to Austin. Transferred there for a year."

But I couldn't afford to stay, and when I crawled back with my tail between my legs . . .

"When I came back, I saw them. They were eating at the Finer Diner with another couple. Laughing. Having a grand ol' time. It's like I never existed. So I set out to make the feeling mutual. I've seen them since then, can't avoid people in a town this small, but I've been able to avoid any kind of direct contact until . . ."

"Until tonight."

I tilt my head. "Recently, it's been harder."

“Well it just goes to show, you have excellent avoidance capabilities if you’ve been able to elude them in a town this small for four years.”

I laugh. “Yeah, I’m real talented in the run-and-hide arena.”

“I’ve noticed.”

My smile falters. “They’re getting married.”

“Does that bother you?” His voice is hushed and quiet, probing but not demanding.

I take stock of the carefully held-back emotions hiding in the cave I’ve put them in, just like the box of photos in the closet. The same ones that were churning earlier. The box has been damaged by my confession and they’re easier to sort. They’ve settled down to smaller, more manageable piles now that I’ve unleashed everything all over Jude.

It’s not jealousy, not like that. I haven’t had romantic feelings for Chad in a long time. It’s been years since I realized I didn’t really love him, I loved the idea of him. The idea of falling in love with my best friend, the idea of having an epic romance. Just like my parents and grandparents and everyone else, and then when the dream was shattered into pieces, no one could make me believe in any of it.

“Not really. You know, once I got over the shock of it all, I wasn’t mad at them. More embarrassed. Ashamed. I felt so stupid that I hadn’t seen it. And by then so much time had passed and it was too late to go back. It was hard, though, for a long time. I was like a zombie. A shell. I didn’t know what to do. Losing Taylor and Chad was like losing my right arm but I couldn’t be around them and watch them love each other. I was the third wheel in the worst of ways, the third wheel who was pining for one of the wheels while it humped the other wheel."

"How did you move on?"

"Writing helped." The words fall out without conscious thought and I wish I could take them back because Jude is too clever to miss the subtext.

"Writing? Not journalism, though."

"No. I . . ." I can't share this with him. Can I? "I started taking writing courses after everything. While I was in Austin. They have a creative writing MFA I was interested in. I had no one to talk to about what I was going through, and writing was the only outlet. I wrote terrible poetry and angst-filled flash fiction and it was like a drug. It was the only way to get the shame out. I originally wanted to major in creative writing, actually."

"Then why the switch to journalism? It's not nearly the same thing."

"It's not." I can't go on.

Of course he can read me like a damn book. "Did something happen that made you feel like you couldn't pursue it as a career?"

"Well . . . it's not easy to find a job or make money to support yourself on something creative."

"True. Doesn't mean it's not a worthy pursuit."

"I was no good at it anyway."

"Why would you think that?"

"Oh, you know, in class we would have critique groups and . . . the professors at UT . . ." I shrug. "No one liked it."

"But that's merely a few opinions. Surely you shared your work with people who know you, like family."

"One professor told me I would be more likely to win the Olympic gold medal in curling than to get published. I tried to prove him wrong. I submitted my work all over the place, but I just got one rejection after another. To the point that I was spending all my time chasing a pipe dream and none working a real job to pay the rent."

"But what about Fitz? Your parents?"

I laugh. "I can't share things with them."

"Why not? They're . . . you and Fitz come from a good family."

"They are good, it's just that, well, Fitz would not want to read about my angsty love life and my parents, that's a little more complicated. We didn't exactly have it all easy, growing up. Money was tight. Don't get me wrong, they're great people, but Daddy was always working, and when I would vent to Momma about my problems, or when I was upset, she would take everything inside her and it would hurt. She cares so much, too much. Once I realized she shared my pain, I didn't want to wear her down. Momma's not strong enough."

Which is why I've been avoiding her calls. But it's more than just that. It's also the shame of one failure after another. If I can't even keep a paying job writing here in Blue Falls, what hope do I have elsewhere?

He sits back. "You've had no one to open up to. Damn near your whole life you kept your true feelings under wraps and every time you opened up to anyone, you experienced rejection in some form. Whether it was your mother, your best friends, the people who were supposed to care about you the most, strangers . . . everyone. No wonder."

"No wonder what?"

"No wonder you've built a hard shell. If you keep yourself hidden, you can't get hurt."

My chest constricts. My eyes water without my permission. "That's not true."

"Isn't it?"

Is he right? I don't know if I can handle all this truth.

His eyes are watching my face now intently, purposefully, like he can see into my soul, especially when he speaks. "All of this is why you don't believe in love."

I roll my eyes. "Not this again. I'm not like Fitz. He's an eternal idealist."

"Well, then explain your parents' relationship. I've heard the story of their epic romance more than a few times from your brother."

"That's different. They're a one-off. It happens, but it's like lightning in a bottle. It's two personalities that can cohabitate, not magic. I'm not my parents. I don't need an epic love, I only need myself."

He nods once. "You're right."

"I am? You're not going to argue with me?"

"I'm only going to say that you can be alone, of course. But you can't escape life forever. Humans are social creatures. You will suffer without connection. And with connection comes pain and vulnerability. It's life. And trust me when I tell you that pain is better than nothing at all."

"You sound like Reese."

"She's a smart lady."

"You can have love and affection without the romance."

"You know what I think? You don't want the pain of rejection ever again and it's made you think romantic love makes you dependent, but it's not like that. Love isn't about relying solely on another for happiness. It's about sharing joy and pain and all of it together. Making each other stronger. Just like friends. Like Reese. She doesn't suck your life away or make you miserable, she makes you better. You think if love doesn't exist, that makes you safe, but what if that belief is keeping you from something great?"

Gone is the Jude I'm used to seeing. There's no joking, no lazy grin or upturned lips. He's serious and his eyes are the deep blue of a calm sea.

Too many emotions. They make my next words sharper.

"Something great," I scoff. "What, like something with you?"

"I have nothing to do with it."

"You're right, you don't. It's simple science and hormones and you're talking about emotion."

"Emotion is part of the human condition."

"Well I don't think it has to be."

"I think it does."

"Why? Enlighten me, oh superior one."

"Here's the thing, Annabel." He leans down so we're on a closer level, his eyes burning into mine. "You are lovable." He says the words with so much sincerity and conviction, it's uncomfortable.

I squirm inwardly. I want to drag my eyes away, but I

can't. He's holding me there like a bug trapped under a glass.

My heart pounds in my ears. "What are you talking about? Don't change the subject."

"It's not that you don't believe love exists, it's that you don't believe in it for you. Because of your experiences, you feel inherently unlovable, so it's safer to say there is no romantic love than to believe it won't happen for you."

I shake my head. "You're wrong."

"Then prove it. Conduct an experiment to test your hypothesis."

"How am I supposed to do that?"

He sits back, making sure to hold my eyes with his. "Be with me."

"What? What are you talking about? You reject me all the time."

"No. I have never rejected you. I just want more from you than what you've been willing to give. I'm not talking about slaking your primitive urges with a one-night stand. I want more than that. Be with me. Date me. I want to take you out to dinner and pick you up and bring you flowers. You shared with me your shame, and I'm still here and willing. I will read your poetry and angst-filled stories and I won't ridicule or condemn you. Trust me. Let's be more than lust. Let's be friends."

"You're kidding."

His eyes are bright blue and intense on mine. "I'm not kidding. You know I'm not, but you want to pretend and joke like you always do because it makes you feel safer."

Anger is bubbling inside me. "That's not true."

"Then again I say, prove it."

How does he expect me to do such a thing? I can't prove it that way. He's such a jerk. I hate him.

Emotions stew inside me, a volcano about to erupt. He's sitting there, calm and still and frustrating as all get out. I can prove him wrong.

I grab his face, lean forward, and kiss him.

Chapter Thirteen

He stepped down, trying not to look long at her as if she were the sun, yet he saw her, like the sun, even without looking.

—Leo Tolstoy, *Anna Karenina*

Jude

ANNABEL IS KISSING ME, and I didn't expect it. My past has taught me how to read people, but I can never predict her. She's the one thing I've never been prepared for.

The action may be just as surprising to her because at first, there is no movement. We're sitting there, our mouths pressed together, her hands on either side of my face. But then her mouth moves against mine, lips parting. Her tongue slips in and my mouth parts without thought and everything else disappears, every external sound, every open browser tab in my mind. The screen goes black.

My arms go around her, pulling her closer. She swings one leg over my lap and then her mouth is back on mine and her tongue is in my mouth and I fall backward onto the bed, taking her with me. This kiss is everything I had built up in my mind and more since the last time her lips were on mine. The reality is so much better than I remembered.

She's on top, in control, but I have some tricks up my sleeve. I lick into her mouth and she's soft and sweet and open. My fingertips trail up her thigh.

She groans and presses down on me, releasing my mouth on a gasp and arching her neck, giving me perfect access. My mouth moves to her neck and she murmurs something unintelligible and I should stop. This is going too fast and she's trying to make me believe this is nothing more than a monkey mating dance, but I can't stop.

She's in my arms and I've been waiting for this for too long. Living with only a memory for too long.

I find that spot on her neck just under her ear and lick it and she moans and squirms against me. She's perfection under my mouth and hands. The little sounds she makes send chills streaming up my arms and my heart thumping faster in my chest. I'm as hard as a rock.

She's perfect—like every piece of her was made especially for me and me for her. The curve of her thigh was molded for the arch of my hand, her tongue was made to slide against mine, the moan in her throat to set off an ache in my chest.

Her hands are on either side of my head, holding

herself up. One hand moves to my shoulder, clutching at me.

I slide one hand higher, under her skirt, chasing the line of her panties, trailing a finger around to her inner thigh. She gasps as I trace her heat through the thin barrier of fabric. Her hips move against my hand, begging for more without saying a word. She's already so wet, and the knowledge makes me groan into her neck.

I might lose it before this can go any further.

Using both hands now, I slide down her underwear far enough to reach inside and run a knuckle along her seam. She moans above me, and then her eyes open and lock on mine, hot and intense, and when I press my thumb to her clit, her eyes fall shut and she groans.

"Jude, please," she pants.

Using one hand, I rub against her wetness, varying my strokes between gentle and firm. Her dress is gaping open at the top and with my free hand, I reach into her falling neckline and my hand stills. She's not wearing a bra.

"Fuck."

I'm not one to swear, but the word falls from my lips anyway. My hand moves faster against her wetness. I push down the dress and lean up, sucking one hardened pink nipple into my mouth and she loses the last thread of her control, grinding and spasming against my hand, arching in her release.

I expect her to be satisfied and collapse into a heap against me. I'm actually looking forward to it, the weight of her in my arms, spent and relieved. But again, she surprises me. Instead of melting into a puddle of orgasmic bliss, she's energized, reaching into my pants, wrapping warm fingers around my hard length.

"Wait." I grab her wrist to stop her motions. It's one thing for me to take care of her and her needs but she doesn't want me. Not really. Not the way I want.

"Please, Jude." Her voice is a low moan that echoes down into my toes and I nearly relent but then she says, in almost a whisper, "Make me forget everything."

Hard no.

I roll over, leaving her on her back on the bed, and then stand up, even though it just about kills me to do so.

She sits on the bed, her face both endearing and heartbreaking. She's watching me with shock and arousal smothered in embarrassment and I can't.

"Not like this," I explain. With one quick step, I'm in front of her, even though it might kill me to touch her again. I cup her face in my hands, her skin soft as silk under my fingers. "Not when you're trying to escape the world. When we're together, I want you to be here. With me. Not running from the past."

Her face is flushed with arousal and she pulls back and out of my reach, eyes darting away. "Most guys wouldn't care." Her tone is snide, carrying the weight of her humiliation. Her nostrils flare, her arms wrap around herself, thoughts moving through her as she overanalyzes my every action and word.

"Annabel." I wait until she reluctantly meets my gaze, her eyes moving to mine even as her head tilts away. I crouch so we are at eye level, placing my hands on either side of her legs, not touching. "I'm not most guys. You know how I feel. I like you. I want this to be real between us, not some fling."

Her shoulders droop, the fight going out of her. She turns to me more fully. "I can't be someone's person."

"I don't believe that, but I can't make you believe it, either. You need to know you're worth the effort."

"I don't want to stay in Blue Falls forever."

"I would never keep you from your dreams, darlin'. That's not how this works."

"Then how does it work?"

"Just like anything else, I imagine. I'm not asking you for anything you're uncomfortable with. I want to be here for you, however you need me."

She pulls away, walls re-erected. "How do you always know what to say? It's like you know exactly how I feel."

"Because I understand what it's like to not be able to trust the people who are supposed to be closest to you. I know about hiding your true self because no one understands you. Our stories aren't the same, not even close, but the emotions are. We all experience loss of faith, shame and suffering, tragedy and hope. No two experiences are exactly the same, but our humanity underneath the experience is identical. And the most beautiful part of it is that, having suffered, you can understand another's suffering. My suffering gave me a gift. It allowed me to see you."

Her eyes are shiny with unspent tears.

"Let me help you, the way Beast and Grace helped me."

She blinks away the tears. "They saved you?"

"No. I saved myself. But they helped because they listened to me and understood me and accepted me as I am. If you want to know the real truth, it all started with Mr. Bojangles."

She laughs and then sniffs and wipes at her nose.

"I told you how I got him from the shelter. Grace actually got him for me. As soon as I picked him up, he put his little head on my shoulder and started purring. I was a goner. I had something worth fighting for. Beast and Grace . . . they're better than any family I have because I chose them. I want to choose you."

She blinks rapidly and I worry I've pushed too hard, too soon. She stands and turns away from me, wiping her eyes and taking a deep breath I only get to witness from behind.

Then she spins back to face me. "Are you staying the night, then? I mean just to sleep. I wouldn't want to offend your delicate sensibilities by suggesting anything further."

A grin tugs at my lips. If she's teasing, she's okay. "That's a mighty fine offer. I would be pleased to take advantage of your hospitality. And your couch."

She smiles, a small stretch of her lips, but my heart nearly stops in my chest all the same.

I want to see more of those smiles. Real ones. Sincere smiles that are so big they leave an afterglow behind.

She gets me a pillow and blanket and I make myself comfortable on her small, lumpy couch. It's about as comfortable as mine, and I smile, remembering how I made Fitz and Reese take turns on my own crappy furniture. Turnabout is fair play, I suppose.

Annabel says good night and disappears into her room and I lie in the quiet darkness, remembering her in my arms and hoping she'll find her way back there again. My mind runs through everything I said and did. What if they weren't the right words? Did I pressure her by giving into her kisses and caresses? I take a deep breath. Those thoughts are for another day.

I toss around ideas for trapping David and fall asleep thinking about the games we play in life, the ones with stakes and the ones without.

THE NEXT MORNING, I'm awoken by the sound of Annabel moving about the kitchen, liquid dribbling into a carafe, and the smell of coffee filling the air.

"It's going to be fine, Momma. Please don't worry." Her voice is low and placating. "I know I should have called, but I didn't want you to worry. Especially because there's nothing to worry about. I've got it handled."

There's a pause and her voice ebbs and flows over me as she moves about the kitchen, turning back and forth. Pacing. I don't want to eavesdrop, but I can't avoid it, either.

"Yes, I'm sure. Fitz and I will be fine. I'll get another job if I have to, but I won't have to. I promise."

More silence except for the creaking linoleum under her feet.

"I know I can talk to you. I know that, Momma, but I don't want you to stress over nothing."

Pause.

"I love you, too. Give Daddy my love."

I haul my creaky joints from the uncomfortable confines of the sofa and find her staring at the coffee pot, her back to me, wearing a thin blue robe, her blonde hair pulled back in a messy bun. Her shoulders are tense.

"Morning." My voice is rumbly with sleep.

She whirls. "Good morning." She fiddles with her robe, her eyes downcast.

I approach carefully, standing next to her, and we watch the pot fill together. "Are you okay?" I have to ask. It couldn't have been easy for her to reach out to her momma after everything she shared last night, but she did it anyway.

The ever-present tension is still between us, but it feels different this morning. It's not hostile and fraught with tension, it's . . . fragile.

Her soft brown eyes lift to mine and she nods and smiles. "It had to be done."

"I'm proud of you."

Pink infuses her cheeks, and the corner of her lip tilts up even as she turns from me to grab a couple of mugs from the cupboard. "Sorry if the talking woke you up. Momma called and I just decided—" She swallows and meets my eyes. "I decided I should talk to her. I avoided all the fussing, thinking it would ease her worries, but in reality it's doing the opposite."

"I bet she feels much better having talked with you. And for the record, you and Fitz will be just fine. I have no doubts about your abilities."

She smiles at me and it's like the sun has broken through the clouds and the storm has passed.

She clears her throat. "So how are we gonna get information from this David guy?"

A slow grin spreads across my face. "I have an idea."

Chapter Fourteen

Generally, by the time you are Real, most of your hair has been loved off, and your eyes drop out and you get loose in your joints and very shabby. But these things don't matter at all, because once you are Real you can't be ugly, except to people who don't understand.

—Margery Williams, *The Velveteen Rabbit*

Annabel

"THE STARS at night are big and bright," Jude sings into the megaphone.

Clap, clap, clap, clap. As one, the crowd in the backyard erupts. "Deep in the heart of Texas!"

I shake my head and laugh through the whoops and hollers of the assembled party.

"Babies! Welcome to the first ever Jude Parker Murder Mystery Evening Extravaganza!"

The cheers swell and flow, like they're the tide and he's the moon controlling them with the pull of his gravitational force.

They are all dressed up for the party, Jude included. He's wearing the bow tie again and he even put the glasses on—which he normally only wears when he's working on his computer. I think he's trying to kill me.

"Tonight is a night unlike any other. Tonight there will be . . . a murder."

An ominous chorus of hums interspersed with laughter.

"That's right, it's quite terrifying. At a point early in the evening, the lights will go out. Don't be scared, babies, it's part of the game. When the lights resume, one of your compatriots will be prostrate. Do me a favor and refrain from calling the authorities as this is a part of the game and none of my babies will be injured during the course of the evening. In the crowd tonight are players who know the story and the events that will play out. They are not participating in the event itself, but will be placing clues throughout the yard. Keep your eyes peeled for the pink envelopes because that's where you will locate the evidence needed to win.

"Your job, ladies and gentlemen, is to observe your fellow partygoers. Pay close attention, my friends, because there will be clues and hints to find throughout the night. You must find the killer. Once you think you have unmasked the villain's identity, submit your findings to Mr. Fitz Moreland." He motions to Fitz, who's standing next to Reese off to the side. Fitz waves and the crowd claps. "The first to piece together the clues correctly and find the murderer will be the champion of the night . . . and the recipient of a nice pot of money. Good night, and good luck!"

Jude is swallowed by the crowd. I keep one eye on him and one on the rest of the party, observing the crowd of scantily clad coeds. I half wish I had worn something more scandalous instead of a simple black dress—the fanciest thing I own. In my granny clothes, I stick out like an orangutan amid sleek little meerkats.

Jude works the crowd, as he does. People shake his hand, clap him on the back, surround him like adoring puppies. He smiles and talks, making them laugh, putting on a show. A shimmer of appreciation tickles its way down my spine. Memories of the other night play in my mind, making my body tighten. The heat of his eyes, his mouth on my breast, and his fingers in my—

Is it hot out here tonight, or is it just him?

I scan the crowd and find David rubbing the shoulders of a lithe redhead in a sequined prom dress and whispering in her ear.

Jude already set it up so David will be the first victim, which means no one will be surprised when he's not around for a few hours.

It was almost too easy. He jumped at the chance to be a part of one of Jude's games. Jude also promised him a cut of the take for the night, so that helped, I'm sure.

Across the yard, Fitz is with Reese. He's pulling her behind a bush in the back. Probably to make out.

Kinda cute, actually, since Reese loves those bushes.

My lips curve up. Huh. I'm not totally grossed out by their romance for once. That's weird.

And damn my eyes, but on that thought, they rove right back over to Jude. He's surrounded by a trio of ladies in short dresses with plunging necklines. They're standing really close to him. Too close. One of them runs a red-tipped finger over his shoulder and down his arm.

I glance away, ignoring the sudden sharpness in my chest. It's none of my never mind.

Beast is in the other corner of the yard opposite me. His arms are crossed over his chest and he's doing what he does best, watching and menacing. He's got the remote that will kill the lights when it's time. I glance down at my watch. Fifteen more minutes of this.

The harem of coeds is still cooing over Jude. One of them gets very close, rubbing his arm, and my ears get hot. There must be steam rising from them.

Jealousy is an insidious thing. Another emotion I would like to suppress please, and damn Jude for opening the crack in my heart and letting out all these . . . *feelings*. It's like the lack of the past few years is making everything extra intense. I don't want to hate on women for being assertive and going after what they want. I just wish they would try their moves on someone else.

Then his eyes meet mine, his lips quirk, and he says something to the harem. Something they don't like. The one rubbing his arms pouts, sticking out her lower lip.

He says something else and then turns, stalking toward me with predatory intent. He stops a few inches away.

"Annabel." His voice is a low rumble, sparking nerves all over my body.

"Jude."

"Are you done shooting daggers at the ladies?"

I shrug and keep my voice even. "I don't know, are they dead yet?"

He laughs. "You 'bout ready?"

"As I'll ever be."

His lips turn up and his eyes twinkle at me and I want to reach out and touch him to erase the interlopers, but I don't. Instead, we maintain eye contact and it's going on too long and normally, I would find this intensely uncomfortable, but instead . . . I could stare at him all day, even with the yeti beard.

The excitement of the night must be getting to me. Or the proximity. It's only because I need to get laid and he has talented fingers. And sexy lips. And a totally hot, rocking body. But that's all.

Dammit, even I don't believe the lies I try to tell myself anymore.

Our conversation gets interrupted by revelers wanting a piece of him, not that I can blame them. He remembers everyone's names, makes comments about prior conversations, or asks about their families. It's like he knows everything.

I nearly forget what we're doing here, lost in the trance of watching Jude enchant everyone, when the yard is pitched into darkness. I lurch in surprise, especially since people in the crowd shriek and scream.

But Jude is there, right next to me. His hand finds mine, warm and reassuring, and I clutch it like a lifeline, leaning into his heat.

"It'll only be a minute, long enough for the players to perform their roles," he says into my ear, his beard tickling the sensitive skin there. I shiver and he wraps an arm around my back.

The seconds rush by and when the lights come back up, he moves away, following the gasps and laughter over to where the first "victim" has met his demise.

"Babies! I hope you're ready to solve the mystery."

I don't need to watch, I know what he'll find: David on his back with a fake knife stuck in his belly and ketchup on him.

"We must remove the body for inspection and autopsy, but we will return with the results shortly. In the meantime, I suggest you investigate the crime scene for any clues."

Beast scoops David up like he's really a baby and carries him off down the side of the house to the garage.

I glance around the yard, making sure Reese and Fitz are done hiding, since they are supposed to help keep an eye out. They don't know what's really happening. They think it's one of Jude's regular shenanigans and didn't even ask questions when he asked them for help. But I want to make sure they're not making out or something before I disappear.

They're at the edge of the yard, watching and talking and laughing.

Once I'm sure everything is running smoothly and all the revelers are busy searching for clues, I disappear into the house and back to Jude's bedroom.

My laptop is still on his bed where I dropped it off earlier. After they confront David, Jude's likely going to have some work to do and I need to start collecting data myself if I'm going to be useful in our endeavors—and have something to give Bruce.

I lock myself in and pull out the monitors, clicking them on like he showed me.

The cameras flicker to life. They're all over the house, even outside and in the garage.

I hit the record button so all of it will be captured in full living color. More blackmail, if David decides to get even stupider.

The garage is nearly empty, just some boxes packed into one side, a table and drawers with tools scattered about lining the other side, and the floor is grey concrete.

Jude has his laptop on the table. Beast is standing in front of the door that leads back into the house, his beefy arms crossed over his chest. I can only see his back since the camera is up in the corner of the garage, but I get a decent side view of David and Jude.

David is glancing at them and then around the room. "What is this? I thought I got to hang out with the keg and some babes until the mystery was solved." He's all smiling frat boy until his eyes trail over Beast, tall and intimidating.

Jude isn't wearing his normal, happy mask.

David's smile falters.

"Your prize is telling us where you got this." Jude holds up the disc.

His eyes flick over the item and then back to Jude's face. He shrugs. "How would I know what that is?"

"Lying is a bad idea." Jude's voice is as hard as I've ever heard it. I know he's a chameleon, but the ice of his tone sends a chill down my spine.

"I'm not lying. Now let me out of here. You can bet your sorry ass I'm gonna tell everyone what a scam artist you are."

"I don't think so."

Beast approaches from behind. David glances back and steps away, but quickly realizes he has nowhere to go.

"I'll sue you for harassment."

Jude twirls the disc in one hand and shrugs. "You're not going to sue me for anything. You wouldn't want information about your extracurricular activities getting around. You just have to answer a few questions."

"I don't have to tell you shit." David crosses his arms over his chest.

"You don't have to tell me much. I already know you've been running errands for someone in the FBI who isn't really FBI and they've been paying you to help them with some after-hours activities. Do you even know what you've been doing?"

David blinks rapidly, his throat moving on a swallow. "How do you . . ."

"You aren't the only one wearing a hat in this town and you definitely aren't the best."

"Oh yeah? Then why did the FBI recruit me to help them?" He's back to the cocky assurance.

Jude is unimpressed. "Really? You think that's who's paying you? You didn't bother tracing them, did you?"

"Of course I did. It's legit. I'm not an idiot."

Except he sort of is because he just basically admitted to everything.

"Listen to me closely. I'll speak real slow so you can understand. The FBI did not contact you."

"Yes, they did," he argues.

"Someone pretending to be the FBI may have contacted you, but not an actual agent. Let me guess, they told you to verify them by tracing their IP to confirm their legitimacy?"

His mouth pops open. "Well . . ."

"Have you even seen them in person, or did they just message you through the computer?"

David's eyes are about to pop out of his head, looking like two fried eggs on a hot plate.

"Anyone can filter their IP through an address in another state. You got handled, and hard."

David's silent for a few long seconds and then his eyes narrow. "You're wrong. There's money in my bank. Money doesn't lie."

"Oh. You mean, the money in this account?" Jude pushes a few buttons on the computer.

David steps closer to the screen, his eyes widening as he recognizes the information. "How did you—"

I can't see it from where I'm standing, but I'm pretty sure Jude has David's account details up on the screen.

"If you don't tell us everything you know . . . " Jude hits a few buttons and whatever happens on the screen is not good for David.

"What are you doing?" His voice is shrill and high and he lunges toward Jude, but Beast is too close. He grabs David's arms and yanks him back with one hand, as easy as he would the string of a balloon.

"A simple hack. You should have protected your assets more carefully. This is another reason I know the FBI did not contact you. Any black hat worth his salt knows how to shelter their money. This is a savings account at the local branch on Sixth Street. It's like you wanted to get caught."

"What do you want from me?" David asks, his shoulders deflating. Not that he has much of a choice with Beast still gripping his wrists in a vise.

"I'll put the money back if you tell me everything you know about this so-called special agent and give me access to your messaging system."

"Fine. Just, just put the money back, okay?"

Jude spends the next hour grilling David on everything he can think of that might help. Every task he's ever been assigned, why Bryce was blackmailed into helping (because David didn't have time and wanted to party—insert major eye roll here), and what he knows about this purported FBI agent.

Usually the tasks are easy, picking things up at specific places and times. He has to be at the "agent's" beck and call, though. Hence the money and hence using Bryce when David had other things to do. He gets a message and is generally expected to act within twenty-four hours. Sometimes an hour or less.

Once all that is done, Jude threatens him with total annihilation if he talks, pointing out the cameras and the fact we've been filming him this whole time, and then David is sent back out to the party with Beast close behind.

Once they leave the room, Jude looks straight at the camera and grins.

Chapter Fifteen

I know not all that may be coming, but be it what it will, I'll go to it laughing.
—Herman Melville, *Moby Dick*

Annabel

THERE'S a knock at the door and I don't even have to ask who it is. I've been waiting since I saw him disappear from the monitors.

I open the door and yank him inside. He shuts and locks the door behind him.

"You did it!"

"Was there ever any doubt?"

"Well, no, I guess not. It was totally badass, though."

He's giving me that slow grin, his eyes running over my face, and I take a step back.

"What are you gonna do now?"

"I'm going to set up an alert so I'll know when this faux FBI agent contacts David. And then I'll see if I can figure out where the money is coming from."

"What about Grace? What's she doing?"

He rubs his beard, the corner of his mouth tipping down. "I'm not sure."

Without thought, I put a hand on his arm. He stares down at where I'm touching him. "You think she's okay? Are you worried about her?"

His eyes meet mine. "She normally checks in every few days, but I haven't heard from her since she set me on Bryce's trail. This is the longest she's gone without contact."

A knock at his bedroom door has us both freezing.

"Annabel? You in there?"

Jude and I share a look. It's Fitz.

He opens the door.

Fitz steps into the room, his eyes moving from me to Jude to the bed, roving over the monitors and tech, then back to me. "What are you guys doing in here?"

I can't help but smile. My little brother is worried about my virtue. It's really quite sweet.

"Uh, Jude needs help with his . . . sheets." It was the first thing that came into my head.

He frowns. "What?"

"The fitted ones are real hard to fold. I was just, you know, showing him how."

"Annabel Lee, you must be outside your mind if you think I believe that." He pauses. "You have no idea how to fold a fitted sheet and I have to fix it every time."

"Fine." I throw up my hands in exasperation and say

the only thing that will keep him from pursuing further questioning. "We're going to have sex. Lots and lots of sex. And it's really kinky. There's whips and cuffs and cameras and other things not mentionable in polite company."

Fitz freezes. Eyes wide, mouth open. "You think any of that is mentionable in *any* company?" His voice is a lot squeakier than normal.

I don't look over at Jude. I don't want to see his expression, which is either as shocked as Fitz or grinning like a loon.

"Yep. We need to do it now, though, because it's the only time we'll have alone and I can get real loud."

He's still not speaking.

"I mean, *really* loud."

Jude nods once. "Can confirm."

Fitz's head shakes back and forth. "No. I can't hear this. Fine, I'll go, and I'll ask no more questions, but I'm still," expression confused, "not sure I believe you. But even if it's a lie, I don't wanna picture it. The party is going fine, by the way. You're welcome for doing all the work here tonight." Fitz waves distractedly as he heads back out the hallway.

"Thank you kindly, Fitzy." Jude shuts the door after him and then turns around to face me. "So. Whips and cuffs, huh? You into all that?"

I shrug. "Don't know, never tried. Might not be opposed if the partner's right."

He glances over at me, his eyes hooded and bright. But he doesn't say anything, though his hands clench at his sides.

A shiver of excitement rolls through me at the thought of Jude tying me up. Or even better, tying *him* up. Heat fills me, but now is not the time.

"We should probably get to work, with all the, uh, geeky stuff." I move over to his desk station, and after a second, he follows.

Unfortunately, I'm not a hacker and I don't understand any of what he needs to do, so I mostly sit on his bed with my laptop and start typing up facts about what we've gathered so far, what I understand about Grace's code—leaving her name out of it—the faux FBI agent, blackmail at BFU . . . Scandal in Blue Falls? Seems like it's more fitting for the *Enquirer* than the *Daily Blue*.

I finish and Jude is still sucked into his computer coding, or whatever, so I open up a blank document and stare at it. I haven't written anything new in forever. Every time I tried, every word I typed was stupid, lame, inadequate.

I take a breath. I don't care if I'm dumb, this isn't for anyone but me.

So I type. I fill it with the emotions of the past week.

The words likely don't make sense to most. I write about despair, regret, longing, shame, feeling fragile as the thinnest blade of grass, all sprinkled with verbs about burning for someone with more heat than the hottest flames of an inferno.

It's a page of nonsense words, not even poetry, really, more like a collection of verbs and nouns and adjectives, but when I'm done, the vise around my chest is only half as tight.

"I've got something." Jude's voice pulls me back.

I stand next to him at his desk. "Did you find where the messages are coming from?"

He frowns. "No. I'm running into too many walls and diversions. It's going to take days to track through it all. But the money . . . this is interesting, because the money is coming through the university."

"What does that mean?"

"Universities are frequently victims of cyber criminals because they have weak security. They also store a ton of personal data, personnel records, and credit cards."

"Damn. I would never have thought of that."

"That's because you don't think like a villain. I can't tell who's moving the funds, but someone is funneling it through university channels. The strangest part is, I don't think the money is being stolen *from* the university like I expected. Their balances are not affected. It's like the money is being moved *through* there to cover their tracks."

"How do we find out who it is?"

He shakes his head. "I have to dig a bit deeper. I also recovered a portion of a message David conveniently forgot to mention from a few days ago."

"What does it say?"

"It was another delivery of some sort. I couldn't locate all of the specifics, but there was a date and location. The corner of Fifth and Main, during the Turkey Parade."

"That's not much to go off of. So what are we gonna do?"

"We should get eyes in the area. Maybe keep a lookout for anything suspicious." He shrugs. "See what pops up."

"It's gonna be hard during the parade. The whole town will be there."

"That's likely the point. Luckily," he stands up and pulls a box down from the top shelf of the closet, "I have some toys to help us out."

Chapter Sixteen

Life appears to me too short to be spent in nursing animosity or registering wrongs.

—Charlotte Brontë, *Jane Eyre*

Annabel

THE TURKEY PARADE is held every year on November 15, come rain or shine or impending disaster.

The streets are lined with people who've been there for hours, waiting for dusk, when it begins. They've brought their beach chairs, coolers, grilled turkey legs, and various turkey paraphernalia. Kids run around with glow sticks. It's basically a big party.

The parade itself comprises a bunch of people moving down the street bearing inflatable turkeys lit up like Christmas trees—big ones, small ones, floats attached to the backs of vehicles. The mayor comes through at the end dressed in a turkey costume and bearing with him Alfred the turkey attached to a leash.

It's crowded and festive and difficult to keep an eye out, which is probably what they were hoping for. Whoever *they* are.

But we take up positions, one of us on either side of Fifth Street while parade goers move between us.

The crowd is full of people who normally attend Jude's party nights, which means he's continually being bothered. He puts on a perfect show for his babies, but when we manage to speak through the two-way communicators, the strain in his voice is apparent. It's hard to keep eyes about when you're constantly surrounded by people vying for your attention.

Meanwhile, I'm the local no one wants to talk to. Ironic, since he thought having a local on his side would be some kinda asset.

"I don't see anything much yet," I tell him through the communicator. One of Jude's toys he kept stashed in his closet, a two-way radio earpiece.

"That's a Texas size ten-four," he rumbles in my ear.

We spend a while standing around on the corners, occasionally speaking through our devices but mostly watching for anything suspicious.

Down at the end of the street, away from the parade, movement catches my eye.

A door opens and a figure emerges dressed in all black. The bulky man in black doesn't do anything suspicious. He just jogs across the street and disappears inside another house.

It's probably nothing. I'm not going to be all paranoid.

A block away at an intersection, a van with tinted windows drives through the stop sign and disappears from view.

Huh.

It wasn't a black van, though. It was white.

Still. Weird.

"Jude?"

"I've been a bit waylaid," he says.

I shift to find him across the street, an ocean of people between us. There's a bleached-blonde head next to him, leaning into him.

"That's what you get for being such a slut," I murmur.

"Hey now, slut-shaming will not be borne on my watch."

"What?" one of the coeds asks.

"Nothing."

I laugh and glance down the road again to see Mr. All in Black coming back out of the house, and he's got someone with him now, someone smaller. It's hard to make out details because they are both covered in black from head to toe. Pants, long sleeves, beanies.

Why do they need hats? It's near dark and not terribly cold. They walk together in the direction of the parade, where I'm standing. I try to act inconspicuous and lean against the building next to me, keeping eyes on them.

It's probably nothing. But the smaller person seems to be really out of it, half carried by the other one. Maybe he's drunk. Or sleeping. They disappear down a side alley.

I hold the button to speak into the communicator. "There are a couple of oddballs traipsing down the street. I'm going to follow."

No response.

Maybe it's not even related. But the all-black outfits are weird. It makes me think they're hiding something and there can't be additional, separate criminal goings-on in Blue Falls. We have three stop lights and not even so much as a Starbucks. It's not exactly a crime-ridden area.

"Jude? I'm following them down a side alley, west of Fifth. You might wanna get over here when you're done with your harem."

I wait fifteen long seconds. Nothing but the hum of silence in my ear.

Screw it.

Moving at a brisk pace, I head to the mouth of the alley. It probably takes less than a minute to reach where they turned off.

The alley is the length of the block, maybe two hundred yards. The big guy is jogging away, now alone, already down at the end of the alley on the other side. He turns the corner, moving in the direction of the parade. He takes one final glance back and I immediately jump into a nearby bush.

Did he see me?

I peek out of the bush but he's gone.

I click the button on the communicator. "Hey, check out the big guy all in black. He's heading toward the parade on Fourth."

After a couple seconds, he responds. "I've got eyes. Following."

"Oh, your fan club decided to leave you alone?"

"You're the only fan than concerns me, darlin'." His voice is full of amusement.

The alley is empty and shrouded in darkness. Where did the other person disappear to? I walk down it slowly. Is someone still here? Hiding? Why?

There's a thump from nearby and I jump back into a bush.

Where did that come from? All that's down here is the back of the houses facing the street and a few sheds.

Did that sound come from a shed?

I move to the nearest one. There are no windows to peer into, and the door is locked when I try it.

Appears to be a simple tumbler lock, no deadbolt.

I glance around but the alley is still empty. I reach into my pocket for a couple of bobby pins. I open the first one to stick it in the knob and disengage the pins in the lock.

I could probably break into this in less than five minutes. If it weren't so dark. There are no streetlamps down here and I can't see diddly-squat. I open the other bobby pin to make a tension lever, but I still can't get the barrel to line up.

I reach for my phone—I can use the flashlight function—but a sound down the alley, a yell that doesn't sound like Jude, has me jumping to hide.

I slip around the side of the shed, listening.

Probably just someone from the parade.

After a moment of quiet, I go back to working on the door.

I've got my phone set up in one hand, shining on the knob, while I use the other to stick the pin. It's real awkward and it's taking too long. I can't twist right with one hand; I don't have enough strength in my wrist.

I think I've almost got it, though.

"Freeze! Hands in the air!"

I drop the pin to the ground and lift my hands, turning my head to see who's behind me. What if it's the bad guy pretending to be a cop? I can't make out much, they've got a flashlight pointed at me, but there's a glint of a badge on their breast.

Footsteps approach from behind. My hands are pulled down and back, and then there's the unmistakable feel of handcuffs clicking around my wrists.

Then I'm spun around to face the cop.

"Chad?"

"Annabel? What are you doing?" He releases my shoulders.

"How did you know I was here?"

He rolls his eyes. Clearly I'm not fooling him with all my attempted misdirection. He still knows me too well. "I'm working the parade. Someone stopped me and said some crazy woman was breaking into a house. I should have known it was you, with such an accurate description."

"Oh, ha ha ha, hilarious."

"What are you doing?" he asks again.

"Um, first of all," I say, like I'm explaining something to a child, "I'm not breaking into a house. This is a shed. And also, what did the narc look like?"

"I don't know. Tall guy. Brown hair, I think."

I groan. "Seriously, Chad?"

"I wasn't paying much attention. I was more concerned about the crime than the innocent passerby."

"Probably not so innocent," I mutter.

"What do you mean?"

"Nothing."

"Annabel, what are you talking about?"

"It's nothing, I'm sure. Just a story I'm working on for the paper."

His eyebrow rises and he shakes his head. "Annabel. I'm a cop now. I think I can handle it. You've always treated me like a kid."

"What? That's not true. I never treated you like a kid."

"It is too true, like I'm some dumb man-child. Even when we were in college."

I freeze. Is he right? Still, old defenses die hard. "You locked yourself out of your dorm room three times in the first week."

He lifts his brows and says nothing.

"Fine. Maybe you're right."

He presses a hand to his chest. "My my my, Annabel. Are you admitting to being wrong? You have gotten older."

"Don't get used to it."

We share a smile, and then he rubs the back of his neck. "You would always give me a hard time. That's why I was so surprised, that day you . . ." He waves a hand. "You know. And I handled it very badly. I'm sorry. You were a good friend. The best."

As usual, my initial reaction is to shut down, not think of or speak of that day, and my face must go blank because Chad puts his hands on my shoulders and ducks his head to meet my eyes.

"Annabel. We were young. Young people do stupid things. Locking myself out of my dorm room wasn't the half of it. I also ended up in the wrong class more than once. And not even on the first day. Like two weeks in."

I shake my head. "Being a space cadet isn't the same as lying to your best friend. There's a difference between idiocy and cruelty."

Chad recoils. "I never meant to hurt you. I never lied to you."

"By omission," I insist.

We're silent, staring at each other, feeling the weight of the past between us heavier than a mountain.

When he finally speaks, his words are low and deliberate. "You should know, I pursued Taylor for a long time. She didn't want anything to happen between us because of you. Although she never told me about your feelings. She kept your secret even though it nearly tore her apart. And I kept my feelings to myself because she asked me to and I love her. I won't apologize for her part in things, but you should know, she misses you. And I do, too. We were dumb kids, but we aren't kids anymore."

Jude's words flash across my mind like a scrolling marquee.

Pain is better than nothing at all. You are lovable.

It's not only about love in the romantic sense of the word. I loved Taylor and Chad, too. And I still do. It doesn't just go away because I will it to.

But I still don't know what to say and so we stand in silence until he finally breaks it, again. "Will you please let her talk to you, at least? To explain?"

A large part of me wants to run away screaming from this whole conversation. But the truth—if I dig down into the cavernous hole in my mind to uncover it—is that I miss Taylor with my whole being. I want her to grovel not because I'm a sadist, but because I miss her so much it hurts. And like a pain that's been ignored for too long, the fix is going to hurt more than the injury that caused it.

"Fine. I'll think about it if you uncuff me."

"Oh, right."

The vise squeezing my chest is now about a quarter as tight.

"Annabel?" Jude's voice calls from down the alley.

"Over here," I call out.

Jude ambles over, speaking as he approaches. "Nice to see you again, Officer."

"You supposed to be keeping an eye on this one?" Chad cocks his head in my direction.

"I think she's pretty good at keeping an eye on herself."

Chad glances back and forth between us, then he grins, his pearly whites flashing in the glow from his flashlight. "This is probably true."

My attention is drawn back to the shed. Is there something here? Why else would I have been ratted out? Who was that guy?

"Come on, I'll escort you guys back to the parade."

Chad's not taking any chances with me. Clearly. "Fine."

We walk with him down the alley to the main street.

"Don't forget. You promised. Taylor will be expecting your call. Her number's the same."

"I promised to think about it!"

He waves a hand while walking off. "And call me before you go breaking into people's sheds. Okay?"

"I'll try."

Chapter Seventeen

The same may be said of friendship at first sight as of love at first sight: it is the only true one, the only noble one.
—Herman Melville, *The Confidence-Man*

Annabel

"WHAT'S FITZ UP TO TONIGHT?" I ask Reese right before shoving an egg roll in my mouth.

"He's over at Jude's." She crosses her legs on the couch next to me, holding her bowl of food in one hand. "There's no party tonight. They're watching *Two Weeks Notice.* Jude really loves Hugh Grant."

I snort. "He loves anyone in romance movies."

Meanwhile, we're watching Keanu Reeves kick some butt as John Wick while we chow down on homemade Chinese food Beast made for us. There are no Chinese restaurants in Blue Falls, but who needs it when you've got Beast?

"I can't believe he made this from scratch." Egg rolls, fried rice, and sweet and sour pineapple with chicken and rice and bell peppers. And it's delicious.

"He's a prince. How is it going with the article?" Reese asks. "Is it whatever you were helping Jude with the other night, or something different?"

"Different."

"What's it about?"

"Um. I can't really talk about it yet."

"Fine. Then tell me what's up with Jude."

"Eh . . ."

"We don't have to talk about him if you don't want to."

"I don't want to."

"Fair enough."

We eat in silence for a few minutes while Keanu murders people on the screen.

"Can I tell you something about Fitz?" Reese says in a soft voice.

I eyeball her. "Maybe?"

"We haven't had sex yet."

Dear lord, where is this going? The last time she asked me for sex advice, she started talking about the mating habits of seahorses. "Okay?"

"I want to, but he's all sweet and doesn't want me to feel rushed."

"Maybe he's not ready."

"You're probably right. How do I find out if he is?"

"Reese. You're the smartest person I know. Just ask him."

"Right. You're so right. Why is this so hard? I'm . . . nervous to talk to him about this, and I can't quite figure out why.

I know exactly why. And the words remind me of the conversation with Jude. The events are different, the emotions the same. "Because telling someone how you feel is hard. It's opening yourself to rejection. But you don't have to worry about that with Fitz. He loves you. Just be safe. Use a condom and for God's sake keep me out of it and don't do it when I'm home."

"Fine. I need more friends who aren't related to my boyfriend," she grumbles.

My phone buzzes on the couch between us.

"Taylor?" Reese reads out the caller ID.

"Hey, Nosy McGee!" I snatch up my phone and decline the call.

"Isn't that the old friend you told me about? The one who lied and isn't your friend anymore?"

"No."

She raises one brow.

"Maybe."

She waits.

"Okay, fine. Yes, it is. You really want to know all the gory details?"

"Of course."

I take a breath. I've already done this once, and I trust Reese, like I trusted Jude. She won't discard my feelings or me. I believe that.

So I open up and let it out. The repeat is surprisingly easy to endure.

The anxiety I had been holding on to was hard and heavy. And now it's . . . not. Not quite as light as a feather, but lighter than the anvil it was.

"I'm sorry you had to go through that." Reese reaches out and puts a hand on my arm.

I shrug. "It's over now."

"Then why is it still affecting you?"

It's not. Is it? I guess it is. "I—"

My phone rings.

Taylor. Again.

I move to decline the call but Reese snatches it up and answers, holding it up to her ear. "Annabel's phone."

"Reese!" I grab at her but she smacks my hand away and stands up, moving away a few paces.

"Oh, hi, Taylor! My name is Reese and I'm friends with Annabel and I've heard so much about you."

"God dammit, Reese!" I follow her around the living room. She swerves around the coffee table and I follow, but she steps over the table and avoids me easily.

She's surprisingly agile and wily all of a sudden.

I grab her by the shoulder and she jerks away.

"It's so nice to meet you, even if it's just over the phone."

Frustrated, I leap up on the coffee table and monkey climb onto her back, wrapping my arms around her neck and prying at the phone with my nails. Her fingers are like claws around my phone and she's talking and fighting me at the same time.

"Annabel would love to speak with you. She's not busy at all, she's right here," Reese yells and then puts the phone next to my ear, which is easy since my head is pressed against hers.

"Hi." I'm breathing too heavy. This is so not normal.

"Hi," Taylor says.

I clamber off Reese, pushing her away as I go and she collapses onto the couch in a heap of laughter.

I hold a fake gun to my head with my fingers, making *shoot me now* gestures.

Reese rolls her eyes. "You're dorkier than I am. Talk to her."

Taylor is speaking at the same time. "I know Chad tried to get you to call me, but I figured I should call you instead. Your number is the same."

"It is. I was planning on calling, I just, uh . . . you know, I'm real busy."

"That's a lame excuse," Reese yells in the background.

Taylor laughs. "Who is the woman that answered?"

"It's Fitz's girlfriend, Reese." I wave my hand at her to shush her and turn away. I can't look at her face while I'm having this conversation. "Ignore her. Look, I'm sorry I haven't called. I'm just . . . I'm embarrassed." I can't believe I admitted it out loud. To Taylor. I'm talking to Taylor, my bestest friend in the whole world who I've been avoiding for four years.

"You shouldn't be. This whole situation was all my fault. I should have told you from the beginning about Chad but I was so worried about hurting you. I kept it from you, and then I kept things from him and the end result was everything falling apart. I was young and stupid. I'm the one who's embarrassed. Please forgive me?"

Well, shit. "It's fine. I forgive you." God, this is uncomfortable. I pace back and forth. "I already talked about all this with Chad, didn't he tell you?"

"He isn't a part of this, it's about me and you. Remember? Taybel?"

A snort of laughter escapes from me. I had nearly forgotten. "I think we agreed it was Annalor. Sounds like a character from *Lord of the Rings*. Taybel sounds like an awkward Hollywood couple that doesn't last more than two weeks and ends with a Twitter war."

She laughs and there's a beat of silence. "I really want to see you. What are you doing now? Can you come over? Chad's working tonight and I hate being here alone and . . ." she trails off uncertainly.

"I'm hanging out with Reese. We have kind of a standing date."

"But we can do something else. We don't have plans," Reese yells in the background. "I would like to meet you. I don't have many friends."

"Reese!" I hiss. "That's not the way to get people to think you're cool."

"Why would I want people to think I'm cool? They'd figure out the truth eventually anyway."

Taylor is cracking up on the other end of the line. "I love her already. Seriously. Come over. I have wine and cheese and . . . I've even got some apple pie from the diner."

Because it's my favorite and she knows it.

Reese is giving me puppy-dog eyes, her hands clasped together in front of her.

I can't fight both of them.

"Fine." I swallow. "We'll be there in fifteen minutes."

Reese is happy dancing when I hang up the phone.

"If this all goes to hell, I'm gonna blame you."

TAYLOR AND CHAD live in a one-story house in an older part of town filled with small families and retirees on a budget. Their home is in the center of a block of houses that are all basically the same, brick with white shutters, except theirs has a porch swing. The yard is well maintained and there's a stout white picket fence out front that makes my heart hurt, only because it's something Taylor used to talk about all the time, having a home and family with the white picket fence.

I knock on the door and shush Reese, who hasn't shut up since we left my apartment. She's bouncing around like a little kid on a trampoline for the first time.

Taylor opens the door. She's got on a nice button-up blouse over her jeans and she's wearing mascara and blush. She must be nervous, because she never puts makeup on unless she's trying to make an impression. It's how she always was.

"Come in, please." She holds the door wider and we enter.

I introduce her to Reese and they shake hands and maintain the polite Southern standard of "So pleased to meet you" and "Thank you so much for coming over" and "Your home is beautiful," as we do.

"Oh, I don't want to hold y'all up here in the entry." Taylor laughs nervously. "Come into the kitchen. I have food and drinks and—" While backing away she turns and runs into the wall.

"Are you okay?" I reach out for her and she whirls around, her cheeks flaming red.

She rubs her nose with a palm. "Other than feeling like a right fool, I'm just peachy. Let's pretend that didn't happen." She takes a large step to the side and goes into the kitchen.

Reese and I follow, sharing a glance, mine alarmed, but Reese is still grinning like she did the whole way here.

"I'm sorry if you're in any kind of pain, but I'm so happy right now," Reese says. "I'm normally the one saying weird things and running into walls."

"Actually, I find it kind of nice, too," I add. "Tamps my own anxiety down to a low simmer."

Taylor blows out a breath and turns around to face us. The kitchen is as quaint as the exterior, with white cupboards and new tiled floors. She stands in the middle of it with her hands on her hips. "Well I'm glad my complete inability to function makes you guys feel better, but I feel as jumpy as a fart in a fan factory."

There's a collective pause and then we're all laughing. If mine is a little forced, at least no one mentions it.

"I think you remember sayings about as good as my granny does," Reese says.

"Do farts really get jumpy?" I ask.

Taylor's leaning forward, arms around her stomach. "Remember when I told Tommy Milner he was so ugly he fell out the ugly tree and *missed* every branch on the way down?"

My laughter redoubles, the genuine article this time. "You've never been any good at making sense when you're swimming with nerves."

When the humor subsides a bit, I'm smiling at Taylor and she's grinning back and it's like everything is back like it was five years ago. Before.

But then reality reaches out and slaps me in the face and my smile wavers and drops.

Taylor sees it and takes a step toward me but then falters. "I have to explain."

Wow, we're just diving into this? I mean, I know that's why I'm here, but I'm not ready.

"That day, when you asked me about Chad, I . . . I panicked. I have no excuse for lying. None. I was stupid and thoughtless and so worried about hurting you that I lied and made it worse. But I knew you would be upset about us, and I was so focused on keeping it a secret it became all I could see. I loved Chad and I was so happy and so guilty because I knew you had feelings for him, too, and I couldn't tell him about you and I couldn't tell you about him without someone getting hurt. It was this strange time because the love I felt was always overshadowed by horrible shame." She's crying now, the tears falling.

I don't know what to do with myself. Do I comfort her? Do I smack her? Instead, I do nothing and she keeps speaking.

"I'm so, so sorry. For everything. Truly. Do you think

you could ever forgive me? I promise I will never lie to you again. Ever. About anything."

AN HOUR and two drinks later, we're sitting on comfortable, oversized recliners set around a coffee table.

After listening to Reese and Taylor totally hit it off, I'm feeling way too good and happy about everything in the universe. I really need to drink more. Why don't I do this more often? Oh right, my liver and basic physical well-being. Man, I'm going to regret this tomorrow.

We're sharing our most embarrassing moments—Reese is explaining how she got mixed up in one of Jude's games and had to break into the pen with the school mascot, Begonia the pig, and put her in a dress.

We laugh and then Taylor says, "This one time, Chad and I . . ." She glances over at me and her laughter trails off. Then her gaze drops to her lap. "Well, it doesn't matter." She tosses back a gulp of wine.

"Okay. No." I set my wine glass down on the table a little too hard. "It does matter. If we're really gonna be friends, we can talk about anything. Even Chad. It's not uncomfortable for me. I don't like him. Not like that, and I haven't for a really long time."

Taylor watches me skeptically and I rush to assure her.

"You know that, right? Stop stressing about it and you have to tell me everything. Chad or not. Them's the rules."

Reese's head tilts. "There are rules?"

She would pick up on that. She loves parameters on

things. "Yes, rules. The rules of friendship and badass womenry." I'm totally making all of this up, but it sounds really good.

Reese's nose scrunches. "Womenry isn't a word."

Maybe good isn't the right adjective. "Well I just made it one. I'm a writer. I can do that."

Taylor blinks and puts her glass down. "I broke the rules of womenry. You were right to not talk to me for so long." Her eyes fill.

The perils of too much wine.

"Okay, okay, stop." I point at her. "No more weepiness."

She stands up and then sits in my chair, squishing herself in beside me. We really don't fit, but she's so earnest and upset, I can't tell her to go away.

"It's fine now. It really is. No shame needed."

She takes one of my hands in hers. "I hope so. And now you're with Jude." Her smile is wide even though her eyes are still watery. "You guys are so cute together."

Reese, quiet until now, speaks up. "Um, what? Why? Jude? You refuse to talk about him with me."

I shake my head. "I'm not with Jude. Nope."

Taylor tilts her head and side-eyes me. "Then why are you always with him, like at Bodean's? And when Chad caught you breaking into that shed?"

Reese moves over to where we're sitting on the small chair and squeezes in on my other side.

"There really isn't room here for this," I tell them.

They ignore me.

"Wait a minute." Reese leans an arm on my leg. I'm like the deaf monkey in the middle while they talk over me. “Why was she breaking into a shed? What happened at Bodean’s?”

Taylor looks at me. “Why do I feel like y’all are living a double life right now?”

Their gazes clash right on my face.

“I can’t tell you guys.”

“But we’re best friends now, right?” Reese glances back and forth between us.

Taylor shrugs and nods. “Okay.”

I smack Taylor with one hand. “Don’t encourage her.” Then I roll my eyes at Reese. “That’s not how friendship works.”

Reese huffs. “Well, I say it does work and so does my new best friend Taylor, and since you’re in this circle, we tell each other everything. That was your rule. Remember? Womenry.” Reese lifts her glass.

“That wasn’t my rule. And some of it isn’t my story to tell.” Even though the booze is giving me loose lips and lowered inhibitions, I can’t break Jude’s trust. I just can’t.

Taylor nods. “Respectable. Then tell us what you can.”

I glance back and forth between them. “Okay, okay, but I need to stand because y’all are crowding me and I’m feeling claustrophobic.”

I stand on a deep breath. When I move out of the way, they collide in the middle of the recliner, shoulders crashing and wine splattering on their shirts. They both laugh and Taylor grabs a nearby napkin, patting Reese on the chest . . . well, on the *boob* with the napkin, which just makes them laugh harder.

“You guys ’bout done?”

"Yes, yes, we're listening," Reese says with a laugh.

I sigh. "You know how Jude said he had some business with the paper?"

Reese nods as Taylor says, "No."

"Well, I'm helping him with that. Sort of. But it's more like I'm helping him find . . . something important, and he's giving me a story in return. We were at Bodean's together because we had to pick up . . . stuff, and then the shed, I thought there was a thing that might be . . . critical to our investigation," I finish and turn to them expectantly.

"That makes no sense," Taylor says.

"What was in the shed?" Reese asks.

I shrug. "I don't know. Probably nothing."

"I know. Why don't we go check out the shed right now?" Taylor suggests.

"Um, because your soon-to-be-husband is a cop and he told me not to?"

She shrugs. "He's not the boss of me. Or you. Screw him. To womenry!" She lifts her glass in the air, sloshing more wine on her shirt.

Reese cheers. "To womenry! But really, we shouldn't drive."

I tap a finger against my lips. It's been a full day since the parade anyway. Whatever I thought I saw is probably gone. But maybe there is evidence left behind. "It's right off Main and Fourth, less than a mile. We could walk."

Taylor gasps. "Yes! But we have to wear all black so no one can see us. Come on!"

She hauls both of us back to her bedroom and throws black clothes at us.

It doesn't work out well. Reese is tall and thin and I'm average height but have a lot more . . . girth. Taylor falls somewhere in between.

But we sure do have a lot of fun sorting through Chad and Taylor's closet.

In the end, Reese is wearing black leggings that are more like capris on her and a black cape that must've belonged to a Halloween costume. Taylor has on a black cowboy hat and sweats and a T-shirt, and I'm wearing one of Chad's giant hoodies and jeans.

I crack up laughing when I catch our reflection on the mirrored closet door.

Reese grins at me. "This is the best girls' night."

We grab some flashlights and head out the front door.

Taylor brings a flask for the road, passing it around while we tromp down the street. The end of every block has a streetlight, but otherwise we have only the moon to guide us. Hopefully we won't need to call anyone for help, because I left my purse behind. Taylor insisted since it's bright and blingy and would have ruined the whole look.

Reese and Taylor are trying to guess about Jude's mysterious ways and what we could possibly be searching for.

"Maybe it's an artifact or some kind of historical relic," Reese says.

Taylor snorts. "Like a Blue Falls version of *Indiana Jones*? I doubt it. I bet it's something dirty. Is it a secret dildo?" Taylor nudges me with an arm, laughing.

"Oh, I've got it!" Reese cuts into the laughter. "Pirate treasure!"

"We're landlocked. How could it be pirate anything?" I ask.

"The pirates could have moved it up here, you know. It's not like the ocean is far."

"Maybe it's a horcrux!" Taylor shouts.

Reese gasps. "Yes!"

"No." I shake my head.

Taylor hooks her arm with mine. "Well, you won't tell us so we're improvising."

We're nearly to the alley now so I stop at the entrance and Taylor and Reese stumble into each other behind me. "It's down here." I hand Taylor my flashlight. "Here. You guys stay down here and keep an eye out."

"You can't go down there alone," Taylor says. "At least bring Reese with you just in case. I'll flash the light if anyone is coming. I'm safer here than you are down there." She grimaces into the darkness of the alley.

I nod and Reese and I make our way toward the shed. We reach the small white building and stop in front of the door. It's a standard knob with a cylinder lock, no padlocks or anything that would cause me any trouble.

"You gonna pick the lock?" Reese asks in a loud whisper.

Something shuffles inside the dark, windowless shed.

"Shhh!" I wave my hand at Reese and we both stare at the shed in silence, our fast breaths the only sound carrying through the night air.

Did I imagine it?

A small thump sounds from the other side.

What if it's a bad guy? Wait. Why would they be hanging out in a shed? What if it's a killer dog?

Hell, maybe it's nothing but my own overactive imagination and too much wine.

My heart is racing. My hands start shaking and I have to take a deep breath before sticking the pins into the lock and twisting, waiting for the tumblers to fall.

Then they do and I jerk my head toward Reese. "I got it."

She flashes her light to Taylor.

Then I open the door.

A figure jumps out, landing right on top of me, and Reese and I go falling to the ground, the shed person on top of us.

It's not a dog or a bad guy. It's a she. A small, blonde . . .

Grace?

She's screaming and kicking and flailing, tiny fists flying, and I struggle to pin her limbs down.

One arm hits Reese in the boob and another strikes me on the side of the face, a sharp pain shooting through my head.

I guess that's one way to sober up quickly.

We are a mess of bodies but I'm bigger and stronger so I manage to get her down and under control by basically sitting on her, but she's still squirming and bucking and fighting for her life.

And she really, really stinks. Like body odor and dirt and old potatoes.

I'm a little shocked and a little out of breath from trying to pin the wildcat down, but I'm sure it's her.

She's a petite blonde who looks nothing like Beast, not

that I can tell under the dirt smudging her face, exactly like Jude said and who else could it be?

"Grace! Stop!" I finally manage to get out.

At the sound of her name, she finally stills. "Who are you?" Eyes blink up at me.

Now I'm grinning. "I'm a friend of Jude's. And Beast. Can we stop fighting now?"

She nods.

Relieved we're no longer in a battle to the death, I swing off of her and then help her stand. Now that she's not trying to kill me, I realize how tiny her hand is in mine. She's bundled up in dark black clothes.

"Where's Beast? Jude?" she asks.

"They're here. I mean, they're in town. They're at home . . . We'll take you there now. Why were you in that shed?" My brain is whirring. Dammit, why didn't I bring my phone?

She blows out a breath, sending long blonde hair flying out of her face. "How do you think? It's not like I locked myself in there."

I look over at Reese, who's on her butt on the ground a few feet away, mouth open, eyes wide. Taylor is standing next to her, panting. She must've run down from the head of the alley.

Someone locked her in there during the Turkey Parade. I glance over at the shed. Someone was keeping her here, clearly. This is the scene of a crime. We might need proof of that later. But it's not like I can fingerprint the place or get an imaginary CSI tech to test for DNA on their lunch break. So, what can I do?

"We gotta get Grace out of here. But . . . we should

get pictures of the inside of this shed." Then at least we'll have some photographic evidence in case whoever it was shows back up—which they will eventually—and cleans up all the physical evidence.

Taylor steps up. "I can run home and grab my phone and come right back."

I shake my head. "No. Not alone. And we need to get to Jude's. But pictures will be important." I grimace in the direction of the dark hovel.

Grace's head cocks and she considers me. "That's smart."

"How did you end up here?" I can't help but ask.

Her eyes meet mine. "I'll explain everything after a shower."

Chapter Eighteen

It's no use going back to yesterday, because I was a different person then.

—Lewis Carroll, *Alice in Wonderland*

Jude

IT'S my favorite part of *Two Weeks Notice*, when Sandra Bullock finally gets her man and orders dinner for two. Fitz is missing it because he's in the bathroom. I'm about to call out to him when the front door slams open.

"Beast? Jude?" Annabel's voice is high and unnatural and I'm at the front door before my brain can register my feet moving.

"Are you okay?" My eyes run over her in a state of semipanic, taking in her figure, which seems to be intact, though it's outfitted all in black with an oversize sweater. Her hair is disheveled and a pink mark blooms on the side of her face. I reach for her without thought, bracing her cheek. "What happened? Are you okay?"

Her gaze shifts to the side.

"Well, shit, Judas Priest. Is this the reception I get? More concerned about your girlfriend? She's fine. I didn't punch her in the face *that* hard." The voice is tired and proud and familiar.

My eyes swing over in shock. "Grace?"

Before I can translate my emotions into action, Beast is there. I'm unceremoniously swept out of the way—along with everyone else—by Beast's giant arm. I get pushed into Annabel and Reese and Taylor as we all bump against the wall.

Beast has Grace up in his arms, his head buried in her small neck while her feet dangle in the air. She grips his massive shoulders, patting him on the back with small motions.

His giant shoulders shake and he's not making a sound and it's still the most emotional thing I've ever witnessed.

"Beast. I'm fine." Grace kicks her feet a little as they dangle over the linoleum. "I love you, too. I missed you, too, but for the love of all that is holy, please put me down."

Grace is dressed oddly, in worn and dirty clothes, which I suppose is to be expected, but the rest of the group in the entry is just as odd. They're all in black and is that a cape on Reese?

I find my voice and put a hand on Grace's shoulder. "You've got some explaining to do, young lady."

She eyes me from her perch. Beast has not put her down yet. Not sure how long till he will. He's still shaking.

"Am I missing something?" Fitz asks from down the hall. "Reese? Annabel? Why are y'all dressed like that?"

Reese slides out from our midst over to Fitz and murmurs into his ear.

"Beast, if you must, you can sit outside the door while I'm cleaning up, but I stink to high heaven and this is making me real uncomfortable."

He immediately releases her and steps back, keeping two giant paws on her shoulders.

"You might need to disinfect yourself just for being in my proximity." She wrinkles her nose and then her eyes run over the rest of us. "I'll explain everything after I've washed my hair ten times. Jude, you got some clothes I could wear?"

"I have some clothes in my room," Reese puts in. "They might be a little on the big side but they'll fit better than Jude's."

Grace eyes Reese, then Annabel. "How many ladies you needin' nowadays, Judas?"

"Oh, Jude isn't my boyfriend," Reese interjects. "Fitz is my boyfriend, and while I do live here with Jude and Beast, I used to live here with Fitz but, well, it was a whole thing."

"Seems like we got a lot of catching up to do." She puts her hands over Beast's, who is still holding her by the shoulders like he'll never let her go. But Grace knows exactly how to make him feel useful. "Make me some food? I'm starved."

Beast grips her one more time, his fingers flexing, and then he moves into the kitchen and the sounds of dishes clanking and cupboards slamming soon follow.

Reese is already heading down the hall and motioning for Grace to follow. "I'll show you the bathroom and get you some clean clothes."

Grace stops by me and smiles, gripping my arm for a second before turning to the ladies still standing in the entry. "Thank you. All of you."

Then she's down the hall, following Reese, and I turn to Annabel and Taylor.

"How the hell did this all happen?"

WHILE GRACE IS in the shower, Annabel gives me a quick rundown of their evening. We send Fitz and Taylor and Reese off to get pictures of the shed and then drop Taylor off at home before Chad gets off work. She agrees to keep things quiet, and they whisper something that sounds like "women airy," but I can't be sure.

A half hour later, everyone is back in the living room. Grace is all scrubbed up and wearing baggy sweat pants and one of Reese's T-shirts that reads *I like big books and I cannot lie*.

We're sitting in the living room because it's the only place with enough seating for all of us. Grace is digging into a giant bowl of Beast's famous jambalaya.

Everyone is sitting, except Beast and I. Beast is standing behind Grace, his arms crossed over his chest, watching over her like he'll kill anyone who gets within a five-foot radius. He even glared at Fitz when he handed her a napkin and a glass of water.

I'm pacing back and forth, holding Mr. Bojangles in my arms to help me think.

"Start at the beginning. Before you left Valdosta. What happened?"

Grace takes a bite of her food and chews carefully. "You know I was working on the trap and track program."

"What's that?" Fitz asks.

"It's a hidden code that basically detects any intrusions and then traces the path back to the source."

"Like a breach detection system?" Reese asks.

"Sort of. Although BDSs are able to find and detect breaches, they don't do anything other than notify the user of a threat. Once a breach is found, work must be done to eliminate the problem, and BDSs don't trace breaches back to the origin because it's often too convoluted to be an automated process. My software is better." The words are spoken without ego, just matter-of-fact.

"What made you come to Blue Falls?" Annabel asks.

"I was testing my code on a system and someone found me."

"You got made?" I ask, surprised.

"They were good," she contends. "But I'm better. They tried to steal my code but only got half of it before I was able to shut it down. I tracked them to Blue Falls but quickly ran into a dead end. They were using a computer at the university."

Beast grunts and I know what he's thinking so I ask for him. "And that made you hightail it all the way here and send us on a wild goose chase after you? Why didn't you tell us right away so we could help?"

She rolls her eyes at me. "I didn't want y'all to get too

involved." She looks up at Beast. "I didn't want you to be associated with me and then potentially in danger. And that wasn't the only reason. I mean, yes, I needed to get back my stolen property. I didn't want the thief to be figuring out the rest of my code and trying to pass it off as their own. But the more I dug, the more I found. One of the IPs I tracked back went through the sheriff's office."

"So? It wouldn't be the first time we've seen law enforcement dealing in something shifty."

"Well, when I kept pulling at the thread, there was even more odd activity. A large chunk of money being filtered through the university was coming from someone associated with the Cornbread Mafia."

"The Cornbread *what*?" Reese asks.

"Southern-style mobsters," I answer. "Started out as petty drug dealers, but they have been increasingly dipping their toes into cybercrime as a way to make money." I turn back to Grace. "You think the mob is involved?" That would kick things up a notch.

"Could be. I think this hacker maybe sold, or is trying to sell, my code to them. They already paid for something with a large price tag from what I can gather."

"Why would the mafia need code that detects breaches in systems? Seems like they'd want to *make* the breaches instead, right?" Annabel asks.

"My guess is they want the code to take down their competition. They've been engaging in digital warfare with other up-and-coming groups, trying to protect their turf. Just like they would a rival drug dealer stealing their block IRL."

"So, whoever stole this code from you, they could be

in a lot of trouble if they don't deliver the whole thing."

She nods. "And the FBI were already here, poking around, which makes me think there are more players in this game than we can see. If the mob or even the FBI gets ahold of my code from this person . . . things could spin out of control. I have to get it back."

I rub my beard. "I get it." Grace is her work. It's her life. It's what's kept her and Beast alive. It gives her purpose. I don't like it, but I get it. And her code in the hands of the mob could lead to bigger problems. The mafia is getting more and more into cybercrime, and data like this could affect a lot of lives beyond this room.

"I couldn't destroy what he stole remotely, so I had to come here. But then I needed help sorting some things, because there was a bit of a pyramid scheme combined with a real lack of tech locally, and it was hampering my abilities to pursue leads."

"Which is why you had us come up behind you to help," I add.

"I needed help, so thanks." She smiles, one cheek dimpling like she's thirteen again. "Anyway, whoever this person is, they figured out I was on their tail right quick. And then a few days ago, someone put a notification out on Nextdoor how they would be out of town for a week and asked their neighbors to keep an eye out."

"And you just had to break in and use their place to crash." A chuckle falls out of me. No wonder she got made.

Grace is sheepish. "I needed a place to regroup for a few days. I don't know how they caught me."

"You would if you'd been going to the township meetings," Annabel puts in.

Grace lifts her brows.

"This is a small town. People talk. There have been reports of someone going into houses and making sandwiches."

Grace turns a soft hue of pink. "Didn't think I left a trail. I'm better at covering virtual tracks than physical ones, apparently."

"So then what happened?" I ask.

"Someone broke in while I was sleeping. I didn't even see them. I was sleeping and then I woke up groggy with my hands tied behind my back. I got drugged."

Beast slams his foot against the hardwood floor.

"Stop throwin' a fit, ya big lug. I'm still alive. They couldn't kill me quite yet since they might need me to get into my computer. I'm surprised they didn't try to make me unlock it for them. Probably didn't want me to know who they were. Or maybe they didn't have time for a long, drawn-out interrogation session. They didn't stop by often or stay long. I never saw a face at all. They were careful." She leans her head back over the couch to look at him. "I think I was out of it for a few days. But then . . . it was a big guy, all covered up, but it felt like he had padding or something under his clothes. He put me in that shed and drugged me again so I slept through most of it. When I woke up, I even had food and water. It was like camping. Except grosser because I had to pee in a bucket. And I think the shed was soundproofed so my yelling and screaming got me a whole lotta nothing."

Beast shifts behind her, his fists clenching and unclenching, and I am inclined to agree with his nonverbal assessment of the situation. Even Mr. Bojangles squirms in my arms and I set him down. He sashays a figure eight through my legs and then hops over to Annabel, settling himself into her lap. I understand the urge.

"We need to get out of here," I tell Grace, though my eyes are on Annabel and Mr. Bojangles.

"No." Grace firms her chin and I know that face. Once she's set her mind to something, she's immovable. "I'm not leaving until I get my computer back. They won't be able to access anything on it, I've got it too locked down for that, but this creep is trying to set me up and steal my hard work. Plus they drugged me and put me in a damn shed and they're working with the mafia. They're dangerous. I'm not leaving without taking them down first."

"I suppose you have a plan?" Fitz asks.

"An inkling of one. I need to know what you found out about Bryce first."

I glance around the assembled motley crew and scrub a hand through my hair. "I think we all need some rest first. We can start working in the morning with clearer heads."

Grace puts her bowl down on the table in front of her. "You're likely right. I'm as tired as a whore on nickel night."

Annabel laughs.

"That's an inappropriate statement for a young lady," I tell Grace.

"Whatever." She yawns. "I've never been appropriate. We all sleeping here, or what?"

Chapter Nineteen

I cannot fix on the hour, or the spot, or the look, or the words, which laid the foundation. It is too long ago. I was in the middle before I knew that I had begun.

—Jane Austen, *Pride and Prejudice*

Annabel

THE ASSEMBLED party disperses shortly after that. Reese and Fitz head back to the apartment, Grace disappears into Reese's tiny room, and Beast sets up outside her door like he's gonna stand watch all night. He likely will.

I don't know what to do with myself. I don't want to go back with Fitz and Reese, and she makes eyes at me like I might not wanna be home tonight with the two of them in residence. So I stay on the lumpy, faded, rose-covered sofa with Mr. Bojangles sleeping in my lap until it's only Jude and me. And in the end, I don't have to do anything because all Jude does is offer his hand. He's like the pied piper and I'm just a mesmerized rat.

Without a word, he holds open the door and I walk into his room.

Only one small lamp is lit on the bedside table, casting the space in shadows. His bed is neatly made as usual, the nightstand holding his glasses and a small notebook.

As soon as he clicks the lock, I yank the giant sweater over my head along with the T-shirt underneath. I'm wearing a cute red bra. It's lacy and sexy. It makes me feel powerful.

So does the awestruck look on Jude's face.

His back is to the door, his hands clenched at his sides. His eyes aren't on my chest, though. They're on my face, watching me with careful intent, flames simmering behind his bright blue gaze.

"Are you sure about this?" he asks.

I nod.

"You know what it means?"

"That I'm gonna be your girlfriend?" I tease, walking toward him, unbuttoning the top of my pants and swinging my hips.

He doesn't smile. He swallows and his Adam's apple bobs.

"What if I told you being Jude Parker's woman doesn't sound like too much of a hardship?"

His eyes search mine. "It's more than that, Annabel. I'll give you all of me and you give me everything back. We both give all we got or it doesn't work. Can you do that?"

I lose my breath, stopping in my tracks. This is hard.

But this is truth. "I'm scared. Which means I can't promise I won't fuck this up, somehow." I run a hand through my hair. "But I can promise I'll try. I won't let you down."

"Just talk to me if you get scared. If you tell me what you feel, no matter how hard, no matter if it hurts, nothing can fuck it up."

His voice hitches as I slide a hand up the inside of his shirt, fingertips sliding over his abs, and he helps me lift it up and off. I shift closer, leaning forward to kiss his collarbone. I pull back and meet his eyes. The flame there ratchets up to an inferno while I reach up behind my back, tugging at the clasp on my bra.

"Don't run," he whispers. "Please."

His arms are taut at his sides, like he's holding everything back in one tight line. But then my bra falls to the floor between us and I lean into him, pressing my bare chest to his, making him suck in a breath.

"Promise you won't hide from me." His breathing gets shorter and I love seeing him like this, flushed and aroused and still doing everything he can to care for me. For us.

My panties get damp and my heart races in my chest and my body thumps in time with it.

"I'm not gonna run, I swear," I promise in one tumbling breath, running my lips over his chest, his neck, down to the tight bud of one nipple and that's all I get before his hands are on me, cupping my face and lifting so he can take my mouth with his, hard and perfect and full of all the pent-up desire he's been holding back for so long the heat of it burns with the intensity of a thousand white suns.

We stay there, near the door, frantic and incendiary, touching until time ceases to have any meaning. All that exists is lips and tongue, the tickle of his beard on my face, his hand cradling my cheek, my fingers running over the ridges of his chest, our bodies pressed together skin to skin.

The throbbing between my legs takes over rational thought and I hook a finger into the waistband of his pants and tug.

"Jude." My voice is breathless and aching with need. I need him closer. I need him *now*.

He holds my wrist, stilling my attempts to get him naked. "I should probably disclose something."

My head tilts back to meet his eyes. *Now* he wants to tell me something? This can't be good. A conversation right before sex is never good. My eyes narrow on him. "Are you married?"

He jerks back. "No."

"You have some kind of disease?"

He laughs, a low sound of humor.

I narrow my eyes at him. "That's not funny."

"I have no diseases, I can assure you, because I've never done this before."

I search his face, my brain taking a moment to make sense of his words. "You've never . . ."

"I'm a virgin." There's no shame in his voice, it's merely a statement of fact. He smiles down at me, his hands rubbing up and down my arms. "Pure as the driven snow. Not much opportunity to meet eligible ladies, let alone bring them home, when I've had a young lady living with me since I've been out on my own." Now it's his turn to search my face for a reaction.

"But the other night, you were so . . ." I remember the feel of his hands on me, how quickly he made me lose my mind. "Skilled."

"I have had some sexual experiences, just not the main event, so to speak. I also read a lot of romance novels, which are surprisingly informative."

A laugh startles out of me. "I guess I shouldn't be shocked. You love those rom coms."

He smiles down at me, but then one corner of his lip tilts down. "I hope this doesn't change your—"

His words cut off because I press my mouth back to his in a hard, scorching kiss. "This makes you ten times hotter," I say between kisses.

He laughs. "I'm glad my innocence meets with your approval."

And then we're kissing and teasing again, but this time he's bolder. His hands cup my breasts, thumbs rubbing over my nipples until they're peaked with need. Then he ducks his head and uses his mouth and I'm moaning and arching against him, my hands tugging at his hair.

"Jude." My voice is full of impatient agony.

"You're so beautiful." His words are a breath against my stomach.

He moves until he's kneeling at my feet and gazing up at me with a tenderness that takes my breath away. And then he's tugging my pants down along with my underwear until they pool at my feet. His hands move around to my rear and he pulls me to his mouth.

His tongue is there, right where I'm burning the most, teasing and licking with gentle sucks and flicks.

My hands sink into his hair, anchoring me upright while he holds me to his mouth. It's so much sensation, I might pass out from too much pleasure. I'm about to turn into a noodle-limbed puddle on the floor but then he moves up, lifting me to the bed a few paces away and setting me on my back. He pulls my clothes from around my feet and returns his mouth to my core, nuzzling, the brush of his beard on my thighs adding to the already intense sensations.

It's so good, but it's not enough.

"Jude, I need you. *Please.*" I'm begging and I don't even care.

He lifts his head from me, moving up my body, kissing my stomach along the way. He's calm and steady and I'm a greedy, ravenous, hot mess.

He reaches over me for the nightstand, pulling out a condom, and as he's stretched out over me, I attempt to shove his pants down his legs, but I'm too clumsy in my desperate movements. I only manage to uncover one ass cheek before he moves back. He's grinning at my clear insanity and helps me shove his pants down and onto the floor while he rips the condom wrapper open with his teeth.

I gaze up at him, from his smiling face down the ridges and edges of his body to the vee of his hips and his hard length, which he's currently wrapping up. As he covers his erection, the heat in my core ratchets up ten more notches.

My hands follow the path of my gaze and then I grab his ass and pull him against me.

My heart is racing in time with my thoughts. More, more, more.

I don't just want Jude inside me, I want him around me, surrounding me, all of it. Everything.

Our eyes are locked, my head caged within the strength of his arms as he slowly, oh so slowly, pushes into me.

Emotion wells up inside of me, because I've never done this before, either. Not like this. Not with someone watching me so intently, holding me with such care, showing me the strength of their hunger with a look and a touch.

The prolonged eye contact should make me panic, but it doesn't. Not when Jude's gaze is so warm and his movements are so tender, pushing in and out with utmost care, the pulse in my body setting up a responding ache in my heart.

My body is so primed, so sensitive and ready and wet, the slow friction so maddeningly erotic that I know it won't take much to push me over the edge. My hands grip at him, pulling him closer. He's watching my reactions so carefully, angling his hips, driving his pelvis against mine, hitting the right spot again and again and again. It doesn't take more than a minute of his purposeful thrusts to shatter my entire body into a cascade of orgasmic bliss. I clutch at him, arching and tensing and pulsing with a mess of sensation and raw emotion.

Once the storm passes, his eyes are dark and hooded in the dim light.

He kisses me gently. On the cheek. The corner of my brow. The side of my jaw. The tip of my nose. His lips are soft and his beard is tickly.

He starts moving inside me again, slowly, purposefully, and now I get to watch him with more awareness. His arms tense beside my head, and he watches me, the heat in his gaze scorching as his eyes trail down to where our bodies are connected.

His head shakes. "I can't . . ."

And then he's all tense, twisting muscle. He comes apart in complete surrender, vulnerability in every shuddering groan and shaky breath.

He collapses on the bed next to me, pulling me into the heat and shelter of his arms.

Emotion reaches out and grabs me, clutching my throat while we hold each other and his entire body trembles next to mine. But it's not the suffocating vise of fear, it's the supportive embrace of life.

I couldn't speak even if I wanted to. I'm too replete and content to expend any energy finding words. I doze in and out, stuck in some kind of hazy consciousness.

When I come to again, blinking my eyes open, he's on his elbow next to me. Watching me. The room is darker, only moonlight coming through the pale curtained windows.

"Are you watching me sleep, creeper?"

"Maybe. Want to run yet?" he asks.

"Surprisingly, no." I adjust slightly, throwing a leg over his hip to bring us closer. He must've gotten rid of the condom. His warm length begins to twitch and grow between us and my stomach shivers with awareness. “This should be weird. Why isn’t this weird?”

He runs his nose along my jaw and kisses me under the ear. “Because it’s us.”

Us.

The word moves down my chest and settles somewhere inside my body, humming with truth.

I half expect his growing erection to turn into more sexy times, but the next thing I know, we’re sleeping.

When I come back to awareness, this time I get to be the creeper as Jude sleeps. He’s on his back now, his chest rising and falling in a slow, sleepy rhythm.

I trail a soft finger over his throat, down the bump of his collarbone, across the subtle ridges of his chest and stomach.

I reach below the blanket. He’s as hard as a rock. My eyes surge to his face. He’s awake now. My ministrations have clearly roused him from slumber.

He whispers my name and the throbbing heat returns full force.

Now I’m the one reaching for the condom, ripping it open with my teeth. I cover him with it and then I cover him with my body. It’s not the same as before. It’s even wilder and more intense. I throw my head back and take my pleasure while his hands roam over me, palming my breasts, teasing my nipples, rubbing where we’re joined until I can’t take it anymore. I cry out his name and collapse against him even as he shudders his release.

I WAKE up to sunshine in a cocoon of warmth and male limbs, taking a moment to bask in the glory of his arms. Arm porn is a thing. And I'm surrounded by it. As I'm appreciating him with my eyes, his hands slide down to mine. He links our fingers and sighs into my hair.

Like before.

I take a slow breath and wait for it. The suffocating tightness, the one that squeezes and tells me I'm not good enough, I need to run, to hide . . . but it doesn't come. It's been fading away and now it's gone.

Lips and beard brush over the back of my neck.

"Can I put a tracker on your phone?" he whispers.

"Huh. This is a new kinda dirty talk."

He chuckles behind me and the movement makes my whole body shudder.

"I can't decide if it's way creepy or way sweet."

"Not only you. I want to put something on everyone's phone. Just in case. Until this is all over."

I flip around to face him in the feeble morning light streaming through the curtains. I'm struck dumb by his smile, his golden skin, his bright eyes, and, yes, even the excess facial hair.

"You're so handsome," I say, like a schoolgirl sighing over a boy band. I am now that person.

His smile grows. "Is that a yes?"

"What were we talking about?" My hand trails down his chest. Lower.

He sucks in a sharp breath when I grip him. "I don't remember," he breathes. "I'll figure it out later."

Chapter Twenty

There are always some lunatics about. It would be a dull world without them.

—Sir Arthur Conan Doyle, "The Red-Headed League"

Jude

THE NEXT MORNING, I walk Annabel out to her car, which is parked down the street. Fitz drove it over here from Taylor's house when they returned the night before.

She has to go to work at the paper, and Grace and I have more than our fair share of tasks ahead of us.

Annabel opens the driver-side door and I step into the space with her, cradling her face in my hands and kissing her with a thoroughness she won't be inclined to forget anytime soon.

She grips my wrists and wraps one leg around mine, tethering herself to me while I lick into her mouth.

When I eventually pull back, her eyes are glazed and her lips are swollen.

I run my thumbs over her pink cheeks. "I'll call you if we find anything."

She nods, then gives me a small smile.

I step back so she can shut her door. Shoving my hands in my pockets, I watch as she fumbles to start her car and then disappears down the street.

I head back to the house, my sluggish mind moving into business mode. I need to get it together, but my body wants to go back to bed with Annabel and not emerge for a week, minimum.

My expectations in that area exceeded all of my wildest dreams and fantasies. There was so much there between us, unspoken but transparent in her eyes, in the way she moved and touched and responded.

Back inside, I head to the kitchen, where we've set up equipment. Beast hands me a cup of coffee.

"Thank you kindly," I tell him before sitting next to Grace at the small Formica dining table.

She's typing away at warp speed on one of my spare computers.

"Any progress?" I ask.

"Getting there," she murmurs, her eyes not leaving the screen.

I open my own laptop and get to work. My mind is absorbed in lines of code and accessing systems, but Annabel is always there, in the corner of my mind.

Hours pass mostly in silence, with the occasional grunt

from Beast as he hands us water and food, always there, always anticipating while we work. It's how we've lived for years.

Once the office of city records opens, I head down there and sweet talk the secretary into getting access to tax files on properties near downtown.

It doesn't take much more than a bit of flattery and then I'm in.

The name on the file is Amelia Quinn.

Something about the name . . . it glimmers in the back of my mind, but when I try to chase the memory, it disappears like smoke.

When I get back to the house and tell Grace, she has more to share.

"That makes sense. I'm pretty sure our guy is Rudy Quinn."

The second she says his name, my head snaps up.

"His degree is in computer science from Rice University in Houston. Amelia Quinn would be his grandmother, but she is deceased." Grace leans back in the chair, watching me. "You know him?"

My head is buzzing. "Yes. I do." I pace behind her to look at the lines of code on her screen.

"It has to be him," she says. "Everything leads back to this guy."

Images of the times I've seen Rudy flash in my head. The air of desperation. The cold shoulders from most of the women in town. "His daddy is the DA."

Grace snorts. "Of course he is. Rat bastard."

Someone with a large sense of entitlement probably doesn't take rejection over and over again well. Men tend to base their self-worth on their luck with the fairer sex, which is a ridiculous and unfortunate side effect of our culture. Either way, he's an unknown factor. Worry slices through me.

Especially when Grace adds, "He has ties to Joe Bickett. They've been sharing encrypted messages. Couldn't break the code to read the details, but the fact that they are even communicating . . . "

Joe Bickett is the leader of the Cornbread Mafia.

My whole world narrows into one thought.

Annabel.

Her cell goes straight to voicemail.

"Track Annabel's phone," I tell Grace.

My stomach is clenching, a sick churning filling my gut. My heart is pounding a staccato of anxiety.

I call the number for the paper.

"You haven't heard?" Jane the receptionist answers in a whisper when I ask for Annabel. "She was arrested about a half hour ago."

Grace is snapping at me, trying to get my attention, but my focus is narrowed down to the voice in my ear. "Why?"

"I don't rightly know. Rudy came in here and handcuffed her and took her away."

I hang up, white noise roaring in my ears.

Grace waits till I meet her eyes. "Her phone is at the police station. Within fifty yards of it, at least."

So he really took her there? Not somewhere out in the backwoods or where there aren't others around? He's ballsy. Or desperate and making mistakes.

Why did he take her? Why not me? How much does he know and how did he connect her to any of it?

I wrestle with a tidal wave of worry and foreboding. I can't help Annabel if my head isn't clear, but when it comes to my feisty blonde amazon, my head has never been on quite straight.

"There's nothing in the police records," Grace says after a spell.

I take a deep breath, trying to calm my racing heart and settle my nerves, but it doesn't work. If anything, the constriction in my chest gets worse.

Think, Jude.

"Chad," I say.

"Who?"

"Taylor, from last night. Her fiancé is a cop. Chad."

Grace's brow lifts. "And we can trust him? Are you sure?"

"No. But Annabel does, and I trust her with my life."

Her head cocks. "Well, I hope you trust her with hers, too. We have to move quick."

I firm my jaw and get to work. Within fifteen minutes we're all gathered in the living room. I called in everyone. Beast, Fitz, Reese, Chad, Taylor. Fitz is barely holding it together, fidgeting and rubbing his face. Reese has an arm around him, both of them pale.

The rest are only slightly better.

After breaking down the essential details, I explain the objective. "We have to get Annabel out of there and expose Rudy for the scum he is."

Dressed in his police uniform, Chad is standing with

Taylor by the couch. He snaps his fingers. "That was him."

"What was him?" Taylor asks.

"At the parade." His eyes meet mine. "He's the one who said someone was breaking into a house and sent me after Annabel. But he was wearing a hat and he wouldn't meet my eyes. He had some kinda padding on under his clothes and he disguised his voice but I knew the angle of his face was familiar. It was Rudy." He shakes his head. "I knew something wasn't quite right about that guy. Always taking extra shifts and kissing the chief's ass."

Grace speaks up. "We have evidence to prove he's been taking money from the mafia and laundering it through the university."

"We can go in there and show it to the chief, then get Annabel out," Fitz suggests.

Chad rubs his chin. "His daddy is the DA. It's not going to be easy to convince the chief to do anything right away, even with the evidence. It will be hard for him to understand the technical aspect of it, and people in this town look out for each other. Y'all are outsiders."

"Annabel isn't," I say.

"But her daddy isn't important, either. Not in the way that will count here."

Fitz runs a hand through his hair in exasperation. "Then let's focus on getting Annabel out of the station."

"But how?" Reese asks.

"Chad?" I nod to him. "Any ideas?"

"He could be holding her at the station somewhere. I have keys if we need them, but we should get him out of the way first. If he's this desperate and armed . . . that could be bad."

I nod. "We need to get Rudy out of the way first, then get Annabel out."

Chad meets my eyes. "Stage a distraction. If something major happened requiring police patrol, we would all get called in, including Rudy. We only have six officers on staff as it is."

"What kind of distraction?" Grace asks.

"Some kind of public disturbance maybe?" he suggests.

"Why, officer, are you suggesting we break the law?" I drawl.

He's nodding slowly. "If there's enough of you, they can't get everyone in trouble. As long as there's no violence. Of course, if you could keep your heads covered, that might be ideal so no one is recognized."

If this were a cartoon, a lightbulb would be flashing over my head.

Grace's eyes lock onto my face. "What are you thinking?"

For the first time since I learned Annabel was arrested, a smile spreads across my face.

"I might know a few people."

AN HOUR LATER, the backyard is packed with babies. My babies. And furries. There are costumes on various clothing racks scattered throughout the area.

It's chaos but it's beautiful.

I can't quite believe this many people showed up as quickly as they did. I made a few calls and most didn't even ask questions. I simply told them I needed them and they all arrived in force.

"Will you help me with this?" Rachel hands Grace a length of yellow fabric.

"What is it?" Grace asks.

"It's my yellow belt."

"Uh, yeah, but why?"

"I bring out the heavy. This just helps put the fear into 'em."

Taylor breaks out laughing, stepping into a zebra outfit.

Granny pops up next to me. "I want to be a fox. They're wily and mean and I like them."

"This is going to be the event of the century," a coed says into her cell as she walks to the next rack of clothes.

"We got any fox outfits?" I ask Bryce.

"Of course. Granny, I got you." He leads her over to another stash of costumes.

Reese and Fitz are helping more people pick out their outfits around the backyard.

"Babies," I yell into the megaphone, "pick your ensemble with haste, please. We head out in ten, and it's gonna be quite the party."

Chapter Twenty-One

I shall be telling this with a sigh
Somewhere ages and ages hence:
Two roads diverged in a wood, and I—
I took the one less traveled by,
And that has made all the difference.
—Robert Frost, "The Road Not Taken"

Annabel

HOW IS it possible that a day that began with so much wonder and beauty could turn into shit on a cracker so quickly?

I stare at my hands on the sterile grey table. Everything in here is grey. The floor, the walls, the handcuffs currently keeping me attached to the metal table in front of me. Even the chair I'm sitting on is grey. Could they not spring for even an ounce of yellow or red?

Although I suppose that's the point. To be depressing. It's like every other interrogation room I've ever seen. On TV, anyway.

There's no two-way mirror, though. But there is a camera blinking at me up in one corner. Surprisingly high-tech for little ol' Blue Falls. I've had a while to sit here and stare at it. Nothing much else to look at.

Rudy left me in here like an hour ago. Maybe. Time is hard to gauge with no clock and nothing but blank walls.

I shut my eyes in embarrassment, the scene playing on a reel through my mind.

I was at work, typing up articles, having a fantastic day, enjoying the delicious soreness of my body, having shiver-inducing flashbacks to my night with Jude, and then . . . and then goddamn Rudy showed up and arrested me.

He handcuffed me in front of everyone and they watched, mouths gaping.

He ignored my loud and repeated requests for him to explain why, exactly, I was being arrested. No one spoke when he read me my rights—full of smug glee, by the way—and then hauled me away. He took my phone and purse, too.

It was terrifying. Humiliating. It must have something to do with Grace. He must be after her. I don't know why he would suspect me of being connected. I haven't done anything illegal.

He shouldn't even be able to link Jude to Grace, since she took so much care to stay away from him and Beast . . . unless he somehow saw us last night? But why not stop us then?

He gave nothing away on the drive to the station, even though I yelled and questioned what the charges were, along with demanding a lawyer and a phone call. He didn't bother booking me. I didn't even see anyone else as he dragged me through the reception area, took a few turns in a maze of hallways, and ended up in this room. He handcuffed me to the table and disappeared again.

And here I sit. Lost in the grey.

I'm tired and thirsty and I really have to pee.

The door handle jiggles and my heart races in my chest.

It swings open and Rudy strides in.

He's the same person I've seen nearly every day of my damn life, but he's different. He's not smiling, meek, desperate Rudy.

This Rudy is arrogant, with hard eyes and a cruel twist to his mouth.

He shuts the door behind him and then reaches up and unplugs the camera.

This isn't looking good for me so far.

He stands on the other side of the table, leaning toward me on his hands. His officer badge glints in the overhead lights. "Annabel."

"Rudy." I'm pleased when my voice isn't shaking because I'm feeling jittery and anxious as all hell.

"This can all go away if you tell me where she is."

I keep my face as blank as possible. "Who?"

"You know who. I have your prints all over a property that doesn't belong to you."

Ah. He ran prints on the shed. Didn't even think of that as a possibility. I had to get fingerprinted years ago, when I worked at a childcare center during high school, but still . . .

"It's not illegal to touch the outside of someone's shed. You haven't explained why you arrested me, you haven't booked me with anything, and you're keeping me isolated from the rest of your cop buddies. It seems to me this is all a bunch of bogus bullshit."

Grace has been involved in illegal activities and it would make sense if I was brought in as part of an investigation against her, but this is clearly not that.

He leans forward into my space.

"Don't make me hurt you, Annabel. I don't want to do it."

Kiss my go-to-hell, is what I want to say, but better to keep silent.

He steps around the table to my side, his thigh resting against my shoulder and upper arm. I resist the urge to lean away. He's a bully. Bullies respond to weakness. I sit up straighter and wait.

"This is the last time I'm going to ask you. Tell me where she is, and I'll let you go."

Without warning, he backhands me across the face and my neck jerks with the strike, the sting echoing through my head.

He got me right where Grace got me last night, except he packs a heavier punch.

"You ready to talk now, princess?"

No, my damn mouth hurts.

My head is hanging off to one side, strands of hair blanketing my face. I take a few breaths through my nose, trying to blink back the automatic tears prompted by the blow.

I take one deep breath and then turn and spit in his face. "Fuck you, Rudy. What do you want with a little girl anyway? What did she do to you besides best your ass? Having an important daddy doesn't make you important. It doesn't make you better or entitled to anything. If you can't run with the big dogs, keep your ass under the porch."

He wipes my spit off his face with the back of one hand, slowly, keeping his eyes on me. They're as black as night and as evil as sin.

My heart races. My whole body tenses, anticipating his next strike, but the radio on his belt beeps.

"Calling all units, we got a 415 downtown on Main and First."

He freezes, his eyes still intent on mine.

A few long beats pass. His breathing is fast and unsteady. I brace myself for more abuse, but then the radio crackles again.

"Unit 33, what is your location?"

He curses, then puts the radio to his mouth. "Copy, 33 responding."

He stands, clipping the radio back on and then bends over, getting right in my face. "I'll be back, princess, and then we're talking. One way or another, I will make you talk, and then I will make that little bitch hand over her secrets."

Secrets? He must want the rest of her code. Or maybe to get into her computer. She mentioned he has it, but he probably can't unlock it, as she said.

"You can't keep me in here forever. I'll scream."

"No. You won't." He pulls something from under the table.

Duct tape.

Dammit I should have kept my mouth shut.

He slaps the tape on my mouth and then leaves, locking the door behind him.

I stare at the wall, thinking. I need to get the hell out of here before he gets back. I jerk at the handcuffs. Definitely not getting myself out of this mess.

The side of my face is one big dull pounding ache.

I still have to pee.

This sucks.

Fifteen minutes later, I'm still staring at the grey wall when the door handle jiggles.

Shit. Is he back already?

There's more rattling, and then it swings open.

"Taylor?" Except my mouth is bound, so it sounds more like, "Mmmaayorr?"

She's already fumbling at my handcuffs. "Chad gave me his keys but it took me forever to figure out where he had you stashed. It's always the last place you look. Quick, everyone's out at the disturbance, but Rudy's gonna catch on right quick."

She unlocks the cuffs and I yank off the duct tape.

"Come on."

"Wait! I gotta take a leak before I burst."

She leads me through a maze of hallways to a bathroom. I pee faster than I ever have in my life while Taylor gives me a brief rundown of what's been going on and I share with her what happened with Rudy.

Within minutes, we're outside at the back of the station.

Taylor's car is there, an old station wagon. Grace is in the back seat. She's wearing a furry costume, a blue one without a head, and she's got a laptop in front of her.

I get into the passenger seat and buckle up as Taylor starts the car and we peel out of the lot. "Where are we going now?"

Grace grins at me, practically bouncing in the back seat. "To find the real FBI."

Chapter Twenty-Two

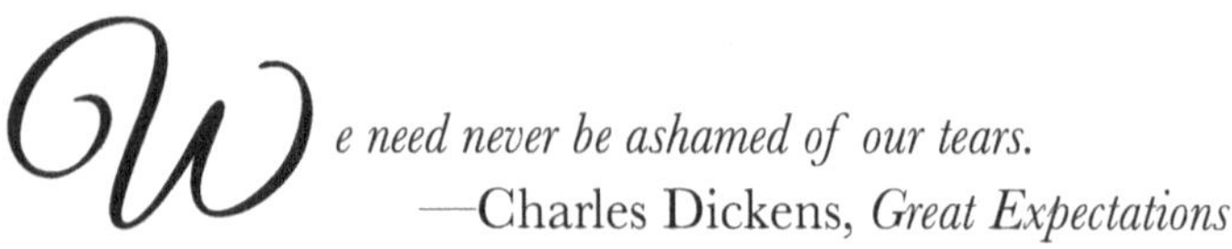

e need never be ashamed of our tears.

—Charles Dickens, *Great Expectations*

Jude

"WELCOME TO THE FIRST EVER FURRY-PALOOZA!" I yell into the megaphone.

The crowd roars. Main Street is crowded with people in colorful costumes for this completely unsanctioned, unpermitted event.

"Ladies and gentlemen, now is the time to let loose and get wild and run free! Let's get this party started!"

Someone brought speakers and at my cue, music blasts overhead. The entire street is slammed for over a full block, and the poor officers of Blue Falls have no idea what to do with themselves.

They aren't equipped for a crowd of this size, and we

have at least a half hour before any neighboring counties can provide assistance. I've been keeping an eye out for our friend, Rudy Quinn.

There's now an officer at each intersection, so it doesn't take long for me to find him when I weave around the periphery.

He's pacing back and forth, talking into his phone, which likely means Annabel has been emancipated. I get close enough to keep an eye on him and pass my megaphone off to a turtle walking by.

My phone rings. Taylor's number. I pull off my furry head and answer on the second ring. "You've got her?"

"Yep." It's Grace. "Annabel is here. She's fine, and we are all safe."

My shoulders sag in relief. "Did y'all find the FBI?"

"I did. Got them everything they needed to take Rudy in. Now we're just waiting for him to leave the 'disturbance' going on down there. They don't want to try and collar him with civilians around while he's armed."

"Good call. I've got an eye on him now."

"What's he doing?"

He's mighty agitated as he paces outside the party near a troop of monkey furries. His phone is pressed to his ear. He keeps glancing behind him and throwing his hands in the air. What is he looking at?

I move around a neon-blue wolf to get a better view down the street, stopping when a zebra prances around me before disappearing between two sparkly unicorns.

Down the block, in the direction he's throwing his hands and yelling, there's a black van.

"Something isn't quite right," I murmur.

"What do you mean? What's wrong?"

I'm on the move. "Grace, be a dear and bring your FBI friends down a block south of Eighth Street. I have a feeling we might be needing to get our friend Rudy and his other friends under control here right quick."

"What other friends?"

"Remember how Rudy has been receiving deposits, and we may have traced it back to folks who like cornbread?"

She's silent for a long moment. "Yeah."

"I think Mr. Cornbread or his friends are coming to collect their product."

"What? *Now?*"

"It would appear that way." If my intuition is correct. And it usually is.

Grace's voice is high and tight. "What are you doing, Judas? Are you on the move? Don't get involved, we're already on the way. There's no need for you to play hero."

"Now now, Gracie, I'm not getting involved. I just want to make sure none of my new friends get caught in the crossfire, so I'm going to lure our friend down away from the party a ways."

"Dammit, Ju—"

I hang up on her.

Then I go after Rudy. Time for some magic tricks.

Annabel

. . .

GRACE IS BITING her lip as she hands Taylor the phone back.

This side of the conversation did not sound promising.

"What is he doing?" I ask. "Is he okay? What did he say?"

Dammit, I sound like a preteen with a crush, which is a pretty accurate assessment of my feelings at the moment.

We're sitting in the back of an FBI van, which wasn't one of the creepy black vans. It's actually a white van with a logo on the side for a stuffed bear delivery company.

Elaine was totally off.

Although it makes sense, black vans are so suspicious looking. If I was trying to be incognito, this would be a better way to blend.

Grace tracked them using their own satellite connection. She made it seem so easy, pushing a few buttons and then shazam. Taylor drove us to their location and we walked up and knocked on the back door.

They didn't answer, totally ignoring us, until Grace started yelling out some tech jargon and mentioned Rudy's name. Then they opened up and hurried us inside.

There are two female agents. Agent Sparks and Agent Ramos. Agent Sparks has dirty-blonde hair and is packing some serious heat in a black holster strapped around a white T-shirt that shows off her toned arms. Agent Ramos looks like a more muscular, angrier version of J.Lo. They are both totally kick-ass.

The van itself isn't what I expected. There's a minifridge and some computer equipment in the back, but it's not super techy or fancy. There's a bench seat, which is where Taylor, Grace, and I are all clumped up right in a row. Not as spacious as TV crime shows led me to believe.

The agents haven't given us a lot of information. They mostly listened to Grace explain the story and then asked a bunch of questions.

Now we're waiting. They want Rudy away from the furry party before they do anything. After all the trouble to get him there in the first place.

But now, it appears that plan has changed as well.

Grace doesn't answer my question directly. Instead, she looks over at Agent Sparks. "Uh, so, Jude's going to get him away from the crowd. He says to meet him a block south of Eighth. There may also be some mafia guys there."

Agent Sparks raises one dark brow. "Okay. Let's move. We're not too far."

Agent Ramos is in the driver's seat. She starts the van and turns it around, heading in the direction of downtown.

"What is he going to do?" I ask Grace, my voice a bare whisper.

She shrugs, not meeting my eyes. "He'll be okay. Jude can be a bit reckless, but he's not dumb." She finally looks at me, casting a ghost of a smile in my direction, but it's small and unconvincing.

She's worried.

The drive to Eighth Street is the longest five minutes of my life. I can't help but go over and over what could go wrong. Rudy is armed and violent and insane. What if he shoots Jude? What if Jude dies? He can't die, I just got him. My stomach churns when I think about all the time

I've wasted avoiding him. Keeping him at arm's length. What was I thinking?

I am an *idiot.*

When the van finally pulls to a stop, Agent Ramos turns to us. "Stay here." She pulls a gun out of her jacket and both agents get out of the van.

Grace snorts. "Stay put. Not likely." She pushes open the back door and races out after them.

Meanwhile, I'm stuck like a horse in the mud. I can't move. I can't even turn to look out the window. I'm breathing hard, like I can't get enough oxygen into my lungs. This is the worst time for a panic attack.

Taylor puts a hand on my shoulder. "He's okay."

"How do you know?"

"Because I can see him right there."

My head lifts. She's pointing out the window and I follow her finger with my eyes.

Jude is there. He's not dead.

He's holding a gun on Rudy.

Or he was. Now the agents are taking over, and he's passing off the weapon, pointing down the street at something.

Grace is jumping around him like a jitterbug.

I'm on the move, pushing out the back doors and running over to them.

Nothing can stop my legs from pumping me to him or my body from tackling Jude in a full-body kiss.

I don't even care if Grace is watching, or that I shoved her aside like swatting a fly, or that the agents are taking Rudy into custody and he's screaming and calling me and Grace stupid bitches.

I don't care because Jude is alive and he's wearing his pink and white Mr. Bojangles costume, but that doesn't matter either because the head is off and I can press my face against him in an approximation of a kiss, but really, it's a major face mashing.

And I'm sobbing. I'm sobbing right into his face.

"Hey, darlin'," he says over my tears, and the rumble of his voice just makes me cry more. "It's okay. We're okay. Everything's all right."

He's whispering endearments to me and I'm literally snotting all over his beard. When I can finally talk, I pull back a little. "You could have died."

"But I didn't." His smile is beautiful. "I told you I'm good at sleight of hand. Taking his gun was easier than sliding a spoon out of a drawer."

My head is shaking back and forth. "I don't know if I can handle this."

His smile drops. "You promised me you wouldn't run."

"I'm not running. I'm talking to you. I just basically attacked you. I'm also panicking. Freaking out. Ready to puke."

He lifts me then, gripping my thighs, and I wrap my legs around his furry waist. "I'm here. I'm not going anywhere. I'm safe. You know, you could have died, too, and you don't see me wanting to turn tail."

I pet his too-hairy, too-perfect, lovable face. "I'm not as strong as you are."

"But you are. You're here. We're here together. We're both strong." His eyes are bright with intensity, staring into mine with trust and shining with so much love.

Emotion he'd been showing me all along, and I just wasn't ready to see it.

"I know. I get it. Waking up every day and loving someone is scary. You might leave me."

He starts to protest but I stop him, putting a hand over his lips. "You could die. You could change your mind. We can't predict what will happen tomorrow. It's uncertain and risky and vulnerable and I'm leaving myself emotionally exposed to pain." I swallow. "But I can't imagine my life without loving you. Without you loving me. That would be no life at all."

He blinks, hard and fast, then crushes his face to mine.

And then he's crying and kissing and snotting all over me.

And I love every disgusting, romantic, pheromone-induced second of it.

Epilogue

The question, O me! so sad, recurring—What good amid these, O me, O life?
Answer.
That you are here—that life exists, and identity,
That the powerful play goes on, and you may contribute a verse.
—Walt Whitman, "O Me! O Life!"

Jude

THE BED SHIFTS, jostling my limbs and luring me from slumber. Lips brush against my forehead, then flutter over my eyes, my cheeks. They find my mouth right as I reach for the culprit, tugging her closer and mentally berating the blankets and clothing separating us.

"Annabel." My voice is husky with sleep.

"Merry Christmas."

I blink my eyes open. Grey light filters in through the

window. Annabel presses against me, one hand on my chest, the other tucked between us. She's wearing reindeer-covered leggings and a green long-sleeve shirt, soft and flimsy.

"Are you the first present I get to open?" I ask, eyes trailing down her form all the way to the Santa socks on her feet. Granny got all of us Christmas pajamas to wear. We opened them last night. Something tells me she'd be scandalized to know what Rudolph can do to a man. Then again, it's Granny, so maybe not.

She chuckles. "Everyone is already waiting downstairs."

We spent all of yesterday at Granny's, drinking mulled-cider moonshine and playing Christmas-themed charades until well after midnight. Everyone stayed the night—Fitz, Reese, Beast, Grace, Annabel, and myself—since there are plenty of bedrooms and Granny was so excited at the prospect of a full house on Christmas morning. She threatened to shoot anyone who tried to leave.

Her eagerness to enjoy the holiday is only superseded by my own, or perhaps Grace's, although she'd never admit to it. We've never had a true Christmas experience. I tried to make the event special when it was just Grace and Beast and me, but none of us knew quite what to do with ourselves, since it wasn't something we had ever experienced as children.

As enthusiastic as I am to enjoy my first real Christmas morning, it cannot eclipse the need for Annabel's skin against mine.

I run a hand down her waist, yanking her more securely against me. "They can wait a bit longer, darlin'."

Thirty minutes and my first unwrapped present later, we descend into the living room. I'm much more awake and Annabel's cheeks are still flushed pink. It's become my favorite color on her over the past month.

Grace sits crisscross on the ground in front of the tree, her red- and gold-snowflake leggings blending with the giant mound of presents behind her. I swear there weren't that many before we went to bed last night.

"Finally," Grace mutters and rolls her eyes at us, but she's smiling. "They're awake!" She yells.

Beast sits on the sofa, his red-and-green flannel pajama pants an inch too short for his long legs. Laughter drifts in from the kitchen, and then Granny, Reese, and Fitz emerge, each holding two mugs in their hands.

"We made hot cocoa," Reese says, handing one of her cups over to Beast. She's wearing a headband with reindeer antlers. "And there's pie for breakfast."

"Pie for breakfast?" Grace's voice ascends an octave.

"It's tradition," Granny says. "Why don't you be Santa's helper and start handing out presents, there, Gracie girl."

Grace grins, nearly vibrating with excitement at the permission to dig into the gifts tumbled around the tree.

Granny passes me one of the cups of hot cocoa and Fitz gives one to Annabel, kissing her on the cheek and murmuring, "Merry Christmas."

I sit on the arm of a recliner next to Annabel, and Grace proceeds to sort and pile presents all around. I watch, not quite sure what to do next.

"Well, what are y'all waiting for?" Granny asks. "Dig in."

More excited than I would like to admit, I pick up the top present in the stack at my feet and rip it open. It's a T-shirt from Fitz and Reese that reads *My other computer is your computer*. I laugh and Reese grins at me.

"Thank you."

She nods and turns to her own mountain of gifts. Everyone is opening at once, tossing the wrapping paper onto the floor. Beast is blinking down at a box of knives—professional chef knives—like he can't quite believe it. Granny is wrapping a colorful knitted scarf around her neck and exclaiming over it while Grace beams. Granny's been teaching her to crochet over the past month.

I want to savor this moment, hold it in my hands before it slips through my fingers like water.

Six weeks ago, I couldn't have imagined it. I wasn't sure I could convince Grace to stay in Blue Falls, but after living here for just a few weeks, I discovered it wasn't difficult at all. Much like me, Grace has craved this sense of family and belonging—of home—even if she didn't quite realize it herself. It only took a few Sunday suppers for her to take a shine to Granny and subsequently want to stay here forever.

It helps that Beast is happy with the culinary school at the university, and she wants to be wherever he is. I even convinced Grace to enroll in a few remedial college courses next semester, since she already obtained her GED over a year ago.

And she has no reason to hack for money, not any longer. The FBI was able to get her computer back for her and she subsequently sold them her product for a pretty penny. Although it hasn't been easy for her to comprehend the leap from scarcity to excess. I've still found her dabbling, but I suppose old habits die hard.

Rudy is in jail, awaiting his trial. He pled not guilty to a variety of charges, including kidnapping, fraud, cyber theft, and police misconduct among others. From what we've been able to suss out, Rudy became involved in his own hacker pursuits when he went to college. He originally got a job in a neighboring county as an analyst working in computer forensics but transferred back to Blue Falls after a harassment complaint from a fellow officer.

We think it was while he was working in cybercrime that he came into contact with the Cornbread Mafia, and it likely didn't take much convincing—read, money—for them to lure him to the dark side.

Annabel squeaks next to me and throws an arm around my waist. "I love these." She's holding up the notebooks I purchased for her, along with some nice pens. "Thank you."

I lean down and brush a kiss over her mouth. She tastes like cocoa and I only get a flash of her eyes, bright and happy, before she's tearing into her next present.

Annabel wrote the story of Rudy Quinn for the *Daily Blue*, digging into the downward spiral of a man who wanted so much to be important that he resorted to thievery and kidnapping. The story hit the streets of Blue Falls and reached beyond, gaining ground all through Texas and the rest of the country. The story included the photos of the shed where Grace was held, complete with pee bucket, which really illustrated the level of crazy to further rivet the public—and the police.

She's been offered a ton of reporting jobs, but instead of taking one of them, she chose to work part-time at the local library so she can pursue her real passion again: fiction.

"Maybe I'll suck at it," she told me the day she quit her job at the paper. "But I won't ever know until I try. And there won't be any success without a little pain."

I smile at the memory.

"Here, open this one." She shoves a present into my hands.

It's a hard, square object, no more than a foot in length and thin around the sides.

She watches me as I ease the wrapping paper off.

It's a framed photo. I spin it over in my hands and a lump lodges in my throat.

It's a picture of all of us at Granny's for Thanksgiving dinner, only a couple weeks after the Rudy debacle. Annabel set up her phone with a timer at the end of the long table to take some pictures.

I knew she had taken them, but I've never seen any of them until now because she told me they hadn't turned out.

Granny is in the center, sitting at the head of the table and smiling with a twinkle in her eye while she watches Beast carve the bird. Fitz and Reese are sitting to the left of Granny. Reese is talking, her mouth open while Fitz gazes at her, a smile curving his lips. Grace is on the other side, already shoveling mashed potatoes into her mouth, having no comprehension of the idea of waiting until everyone is served before eating. Next to her, I have an arm around Annabel's shoulders, pulling her into me and kissing the side of her face while she's laughing so hard her eyes are nearly shut with mirth.

It's a beautiful, messy, perfect picture of everything I've ever wanted and now have spread out before me.

Home. Family. Love.

Annabel grins down at the picture. "Isn't it the best?"

My eyes rove over her face, then over the rest of the people in the room. Granny pours something from a flask into her cocoa. Beast still has a pile of gifts wrapped in front of him but is busy watching Grace, who's given up on playing elf and is tearing open her own presents, squealing over a new backpack. Fitz is laughing, a partially opened foot massager in his lap from Reese, who's leaning over him and pointing out all the ways it will help his "plantar fascia tissue" during track season.

My gaze ends where it all began: on Annabel, her brown eyes warm and full of the same emotion that fills my chest, as if she is the reflection of everything residing in my heart. And she is.

"It's more than the best," I admit. "It's everything."

The End

About the Author

Go here to sign up for the newsletter! www.authormaryframe.com

Mary Frame is a full-time mother and wife with a full-time job. She has no idea how she manages to write novels except that it helps being a dedicated introvert. She doesn't enjoy writing about herself in third person, but she does enjoy reading, writing, dancing, and damaging the eardrums of her coworkers when she randomly decides to sing to them. She lives in Reno, Nevada, with her husband, two children, and a border collie named Stella.

She LOVES hearing from readers and will not only respond but likely begin stalking them while tossing out hearts and flowers and rainbows! If that doesn't creep you out, email her at:

maryframeauthor@gmail.com